The Billy Goats Gruff

Retold by Jane Bingham

Illustrated by
Daniel Postgate

Reading Consultant: Alison Kelly
Roehampton University

Contents

Chapter 1

On the farm

We're the Gruff brothers.

Once upon a time, three billy goats lived on a farm, in the shadow of a mountain. They were brothers and their last name was Gruff.

Beanie was the youngest. He was small and skinny, always hungry...

and always in trouble.

Bertie was the middle
brother.

He was crazy about sports.

Biffer was the oldest. He was big and strong and looked after his brothers.

Chapter 2

Time to go

One winter, there was very little food on the farm.

"I'm so hungry," moaned Beanie, "I've only eaten a piece of hay today."

"Fibber," said Bertie, "I saw you at the clothesline earlier. You ate two socks and a shirt."

Clothes don't count!

Biffer was worried. "I think it's time we made a move," he said. "We'll starve if we stay here."

"Where will we go?" asked Beanie.

"To the Juicy Fields beyond the hills," Biffer replied. "No one lives there, so we'll have plenty of food. We just have to cross the Rushing River."

Bertie looked terrified. "We can't go over the river!" he cried. "That's where the Terrible Troll lives."

He's got eyes like saucers.

And a nose as long as a poker.

"He's huge and green," said Beanie. "He'll gobble us up."

"Don't be silly," Biffer said. "There's no such thing as trolls. That's farmyard talk."

Chapter 3

Setting off

The Billy Goats Gruff spent a week preparing for their adventure. Biffer found an old map to show them the way.

Then Beanie and Bertie
had to learn to climb
up hills.

Oof!

Beanie was better
at coming down.

14

After a few days, they were both excellent climbers.

Finally, the brothers had to pack for their journey.

Things we need
Map
Compass
Hay
Water
Ball

At last, the Billy Goats Gruff were ready to set off. All the other farm animals came to say goodbye.

The younger animals wanted to go too. But the older ones shook their heads. "Let's hope they make it past the bridge," they muttered.

17

Chapter 4

Into the forest

Bertie and Beanie were still dreaming of the Juicy Fields as they left the farm.

Ahead of them loomed the Dark Forest.

"I'm not sure I want to go in there," said Beanie.

"We'll be fine," said Biffer, "as long as we stick together."

The billy goats trotted along the path. The only sound was the tap-tap-tapping of their hooves on the forest floor.

Suddenly, a thick mist swirled around them.

I can hardly see my feet.

Beanie shivered. "I don't like this forest. It's spooky," he said. "Do you think there might be ghosts here?"

"Yes," said Bertie, with a grin. "Lots of ghosts. And more than anything, ghosts like scaring little billy goats."

"Shut up, Bertie," said Biffer sternly. "Stop scaring Beanie."

21

The billy goats walked on in silence.

"Um, Biffer?" Beanie said after a while.

"Yes, Beanie?"

"I think someone's following us."

Listen!

The billy goats stopped and listened. They strained their ears... and heard a thumping sound. It grew louder with every second.

"Oh no," shrieked Beanie. "Look behind us!" A strange shape was coming down the path – and it was heading straight for them.

It's a ghost!

"Run!" cried Bertie. "Run for your lives."

Before Biffer could stop
them, Beanie and Bertie had
raced off down the path.

We've got to
stick together!

"Come back," Biffer shouted.
"It's not a ghost. It's a..."

Biffer waited, as the shape slowly appeared out of the mist. "It's only a rabbit," he said.

Don't be so rude!

"I'm not *only* a rabbit," said the rabbit. "I'm a rare breed of tall, lop-eared rabbit and my name is Buffy."

25

"I'm Biffer. Nice to meet you," said Biffer quickly, "but I must find my brothers before they get lost."

Sorry, no time to chat.

"Where are you going?" Buffy asked.

"To the Juicy Fields by the mountains," Biffer called, running after his brothers.

26

"Watch out for the troll," Buffy shouted after him. Biffer didn't hear. He had already headed deeper into the forest.

Oh dear. No one's ever made it past the troll.

Chapter 5

Tricking the troll

Hello? Anyone there?

Meanwhile, Bertie was wandering alone through the forest. He had lost Beanie in the mist and he didn't know which way to go.

Beanie had been luckier. He had found the path that ran straight through the forest.

Whew! That was close.

"I can't wait to get to the Juicy Fields," Beanie thought, as he headed to the river.

The only way to cross the
Rushing River was over a little
wooden bridge. Next to the
bridge was a big wooden sign.

WARNING

Goats

beware!

"I wish I could read,"
thought Beanie.

30

His hooves went clippety-clop, clippety-clop over the bridge. But as he reached the middle of the river...

...a large, green hand smashed through the wooden planks and grabbed Beanie's leg.

Beanie screamed.

"Who's that going over my bridge?" roared a terrible voice. "I'm coming to gobble you up!"

Let go!

Beanie's eyes bulged with terror. There, crouched under the bridge, was a fat and warty troll.

"Please don't eat me," cried Beanie. "I'm only a little goat. My big brother is coming behind me. He'll be much tastier than me."

I'm sure you'd rather eat him.

"I think I can wait a little longer for my dinner," said the troll. "Now get off my bridge."

Shaking with fear, Beanie
wobbled off the bridge and
went to hide in some bushes.
"I hope Bertie can save
himself," he thought.

Chapter 6

Bertie on the bridge

Bertie arrived soon after
and trotted onto the bridge –
clappety-clop-bonk, clappety-
clop-bonk. (He was bouncing
his ball.)

"Who's that bouncing over my bridge?" bellowed the troll.

Oh no!

Bertie peered over the bridge, and gulped. "I didn't think trolls were real," he said.

"I'm real and I'm hungry,"
said the troll, "and I'm coming
to gobble you up!"

"You'll make a
very tasty meal,"
the troll went on.
"Nice fresh billy
goat. Yum, yum."

"Stop!" cried Bertie, thinking quickly. "You can't eat me. I'm only a medium-sized billy goat. My big brother is coming behind me. He's much fatter."

What big teeth he has...

"Humph," said the troll, rubbing his stomach. "I'll wait for the fattest one then. He had better be juicy."

Chapter 7

Brave Biffer

At last, Biffer came out of the
forest. When he spotted his
brothers on the other side of
the river, he raced to the bank.

Beanie and Bertie leaped
out of the bushes, waving their
hooves wildly.

"Stop Biffer!" they cried.
"STOP! There's a troll under
the bridge."

It was too late. Biffer was already crossing. His heavy hooves went clunkety-clop, clunkety-clop and the bridge strained under his weight.

By this time, the troll was starving.

"Who's that stomping over my bridge?" he roared.

I'm going to gobble you up!

But Biffer stood his ground. "I'm an enormous billy goat," Biffer said, "and I'm ready for a fight."

Biffer lowered his head and caught the troll on his horns.

He bounced the troll into the air. Then, with a toss of his head, Biffer whacked him into the Rushing River.

44

The troll landed with an enormous SPLASH. He sank under the water and was never seen again.

Beanie and Bertie couldn't
believe it.
"You're the best, Biffer!"
they cried.

Just then, a stream of
animals came out of the forest
– deer, squirrels, rabbits and
foxes. In a large crowd, they
skipped across the bridge.

"Where are you going?"
Biffer asked a rabbit.

"We're off to the Juicy
Fields," she replied. "We've
been trapped in the forest for
years, because of the troll.
Now, at last, we're free."

Our hero!

I hope there'll
be enough
food...

This retelling of *The Billy Goats Gruff* is
based on the folktale from Norway.

Edited by Susanna Davidson

Designed by Russell Punter
and Natacha Goransky

Series editor: Lesley Sims

This edition first published in 2007 by Usborne Publishing Ltd.,
Usborne House, 83-85 Saffron Hill, London EC1N 8RT, England.
www.usborne.com Copyright © 2007, 2004 Usborne Publishing Ltd.

Adrian Mitchell

THE WILD ANIMAL

SONG CONTEST

AND

MOWGLI'S

JUNGLE

Introduction and activities by
Alison Jenkins

HEINEMANN
EDUCATIONAL

Heinemann Educational,
a division of Heinemann Publishers (Oxford) Ltd
Halley Court, Jordan Hill, Oxford OX2 8EJ

OXFORD LONDON EDINBURGH
MADRID ATHENS BOLOGNA PARIS
MELBOURNE SYDNEY AUCKLAND SINGAPORE TOKYO
IBADAN NAIROBI HARARE GABORONE PORTSMOUTH NH (USA)

Published in the *Heinemann Plays* series 1993
97 96 95 94 93
10 9 8 7 6 5 4 3 2 1

A catalogue record for this book is available from the British Library on request.
ISBN 0 435 23296 7

Cover design by Keith Pointing

Designed by Jeffery White Creative Associates

Typset by Taurus Graphics, Kidlington, Oxon

Printed by Clays Ltd, St Ives plc

CONTENTS

INTRODUCTION

Although their starting points and stories are quite different, these two plays by the poet and playwright Adrian Mitchell share a common theme – that humans can learn a lot from the animal kingdom but that animals would do as well to ignore the ways of humans.

The Wild Animal Song Contest is an original story mixing songs and debate which follows the events of an international song contest where animal representatives from America, Russia, Africa and Britain compete to win the prize for their country. However, we find out that the prize is the Million Gun, a gun capable of killing a million animals with one bullet. And it has one hundred thousand bullets … .

Mowgli's Jungle is an adaptation of *The Jungle Book* stories by Rudyard Kipling, which were originally written in 1894. The stories follow the exploits of the young boy, Mowgli, who as a baby is lost in the jungle and brought up by a pack of wolves and other wild animals. He is taught by Baloo, the bear, and Bagheera, the black panther, who instruct him in the law and business of the jungle.

Historical background

The Wild Animal Song Contest was written before the collapse of the USSR (Union of Soviet Socialist Republics, also known as the Soviet Union) and the end of the Cold War in late 1990. The USSR was an enormous communist superstate made up of Russia and neighbouring countries which are now independent, such as Georgia, Siberia, Ukraine, Armenia, Azerbaijan, Estonia, Latvia, and Lithuania. The USSR was often referred to simply as Russia, as in *The Wild Animal Song Contest*. The bear in the play, Artovsky, represents the old enormous communist superpower, not what is now known as Russia.

This USSR was seen as a great threat by western countries, particularly America. For over forty years after World War Two these two superpowers treated each other with hostility and suspicion and each side built up enormous stores of nuclear weapons to use against each other. This was known as the Cold War. So in the play, it is a particularly big moment when Artovsky the Russian bear and Quilla the American eagle get married.

The fact that the USSR was a communist country also explains some of Artovsky's behaviour. To begin with, he calls everyone comrade, which was the usual form of address in communist Russia. The communist state controlled everything about the life of its citizens and it is clear that the first song (*The March of the Bear*) sung by Artovsky was produced by the government. It sounds like a song written by committee which expresses, very clumsily, the way it thinks the USSR should be seen in the world.

The Jungle Book stories are set in India during the time of the British Empire. The British ruled India for nearly 200 years until 1947. Many well-off Englishmen went out to India hoping to make a career, often as soldiers or officials of the British government. Many took their families with them. In the play Mr Barnstaple is one of the many minor officials appointed by the government to govern districts in India.

When Kipling wrote *The Jungle Book* stories in 1894, Queen Victoria had been Queen of England for nearly 60 years and Empress of India for nearly 30, and must have seemed virtually indestructible to her subjects. This helps to explain why

Massua has a picture of Queen Victoria in her village hut and knows about her even though she is thousands of miles away.

Reading and performance

Both plays will work well in classroom reading. The songs of both can be treated as verse for reading aloud by individuals or as group performances.

Staging the play presents a few obvious problems. Both involve a cast playing animals and *Mowgli's Jungle* has a setting which would be challenging to reproduce realistically. However, there are countless ways of producing *Mowgli's Jungle* and *The Wild Animal Song Contest* without elaborate sets or costumes. Working out how to indicate an animal's identity with minimal props or conveying the feel of Mowgli's journey with the Bandar-log, without actually having him swinging above the stage is a valuable, and enjoyable, group task. Of course, if either play becomes a major school production and the craft, design and technology and music departments are keen to be involved, the sky's the limit.

About the authors

Joseph Rudyard Kipling was born in Bombay, India in 1865 and was educated in England at a boarding school. When he was seventeen he returned to India and worked on various newspapers and journals. At this time he wrote a series of poems published in a volume called *Departmental Ditties* (1886). He married in 1892 and had three children but he and his wife were to outlive all of them.

In 1907 Kipling was awarded the Nobel Prize for Literature. Throughout his life he had a genuine hope for a peaceful world and the happiness of humankind, and his vivid imaginative writing spans the whole range of human emotion. His most recognised achievements are perhaps his stories for children, principally *The Jungle Book* (1894), *Kim* (1901) and *Just So Stories* (1902).

Kipling died in 1936 and is buried in Westminster Abbey.

Adrian Mitchell was born in London in 1932. He has published several volumes of poems, novels and books for children including *Our Mammoth, Baron Munchausen* and *Nothingmas Day.*

His plays for children inclue *The White Deer, Mowgli's Jungle, The Wild Animal Song Contest, You Must Believe All This, The Lost Wood in Sector 88, Tamburlane The Mad Hen* and *The Pied Piper.*

He has written many original plays and adaptations staged by the Royal National Theatre, the Royal Shakespeare Company and other theatres around the country.

He has held Fellowships at Lancaster University, Wesleyan and Cambridge and has given over 1000 performances of his poems in theatres, colleges, pubs, prisons, schools and streets.

Questions and Explorations

Ideas for follow-up work can be found at the end of the plays. The first section *Keeping Track* comprises straightforward questions on the text to help you think carefully about what is happening in the play. These can be completed orally in class discussion, or in note form, as you read through the play.

Suggestions for a more detailed look at some of the issues raised in the play follow in the section called *Explorations.*

Finally, a glossary provides a useful reference for potentially difficult words, in addition to allusions to people and concepts well known when the plays were written but not so well known now.

Alison Jenkins

The Wild Animal Song Contest

Adrian Mitchell

SONGS

1	Get your work done, son	Debit
2	Song contest song	Debit, Quilla, Rogan, Artovsky
3	Making fun of Raffa	Debit, Quilla, Rogan, Artovsky
4	Raffa's sorry song	Raffa
5	When the eagle smiles	Quilla and the Bluebirds of Mayhem
6	The march of the bear	Artovsky and the Howling Wolves
7	The dancing bear	Artovsky
8	Roaring song	Rogan
9	The cameleopard	Raffa
10	What the penguin wants	Debit
11	Group a group	Raffa, Quilla, Artovsky, Rogan
12	The land of war	Debit
13	New lion	Rogan, Quilla, Artovsky, Raffa
14	The wedding of the eagle and the bear	Quilla, Artovsky
15	Take your turn	Quilla, Artovsky, Rogan, Raffa
16	Bonzo's rap	Bonzo
17	Peace	Rogan, Raffa, Artovsky, Debit, Quilla, Bonzo and Audience

LIST OF CHARACTERS

Bonzo	An ageing dog with floppy ears. Roadie and general dogsbody to the Contest Organiser.
Kingsley Debit	Master of Ceremonies and Contest Organiser. A slick, balding king penguin. Wears medals.
Quilla	An American golden eagle, female.
Artovsky	A Russian bear, male.
Rogan	A Cockney lion, getting on, male.
Raffa	An African giraffe, female.

All characters must be able to sing without mikes and play instruments without electricity.

Set
The frame of one enormous TV screen, big enough for four or five characters to stand inside at one time. On top is a spectacular silver aerial. Beside the TV screen is a dressing-room, suggested by a dressing-room table and a square arrangement of light-bulbs – like lights round an actor's mirror.

THE WILD ANIMAL SONG CONTEST

*Bonzo is working on the set, completing the TV set
and then hoisting up the TV aerial. His work can be
watched for some time before the show's compere,
Kingsley Debit, waddles on officiously. Debit is a king
penguin balding a bit, very bossy. Bonzo is an old dog
with floppy ears employed by Debit. Debit with a fake
handmike addresses the mighty throng from the
dressing-room.*

Debit   Roll up every bird, roll up every beast!
It's a great occasion to say the least.
Roll up every reptile and every fish!
We're going to get wilder than your wildest wish.
Give your beak a shake, give your wings a flap,
Hit the beat with your feet and get ready to clap
For today is a superfabulous date …

Bonzo   Where you want this thing put, mate?

Debit   Stick it anywhere, then hang around.
I'm sorry about that ridiculous hound
But it's hard to find, for a roadie's job,
Anything better than a canine slob.
But now I'd like to introduce to you
The cleverest creature of all – guess who?
Yes, it's Kingsley Debit, your genial host,
The mighty King Penguin, the marvellous most.
There are billions of beings in the solar system
Quadrillions, but there's not time to list 'em
And of all of those, who was thought the best
To introduce this wonderful contest?
Yes, Debit, me! So without more ado
I'd like to welcome you all to
A feast of talent, music and ambition …
THE WILD ANIMAL SONG COMPETITION.

Come on Bonzo, no time for skyving.
The first contestants will soon be arriving.

Get your Work Done, Son

Get your work done, son
Hurry up and get it
Get your work done, son
Or you're going to regret it
Get the stuff lifted
Have it all shifted
Put it all in place
Or you'll get it in the face
Get your work done, son
Hurry up and get it
Get your work done, son
Or you're going to regret it
Better keep going
Or there's no knowing
Better beat the clock
Or you're out of work, cock
So get your work done, son
Hurry up and get it
Get your work done, son
Or you're going to regret it
And you'll never forget it
Get your work done, son.

Bonzo　Right boss.

Debit　Any moment the stars are going to arrive.

(Bonzo looks up.)

Not the stars in the sky, mudhound, the singing stars. They're going to be coming from every corner of the universe.

(Bonzo looks up again.)

No, from all over the world. Come on you doughnut with a tail, get that aerial adjusted.

Bonzo　Right, boss, sorry.

Debit　There's no such thing as sorry!

Bonzo points. Debit's attention is drawn to the arrival of Quilla, the great Golden Eagle from the USA. The

*arrival should be accompanied by music coming from
a distance outside.*

Debit It's Quilla, the great Golden Eagle. She's the
performer from the United States of America.

(Quilla arrives shaking wings.)

Quilla Quilla the Killer, that's me baby.

Debit How was your journey, oh wingerful one?

Quilla Great flight, kid. First class as always. I'm here to say
it's the only way. That Atlantic Ocean's just a puddle
– if you got the wingspan. Had me a seagull for
lunch. Stuffed albatross for breakfast.

Debit How long did it take?

Quilla You'll find it in the Guinness Book of Bird Records.
That's enough backchat, Mr Debit, I'm here to
compete, I'm here to win. When does your little
contest begin?

Debit Soon as we can get together, get rehearsed and get
crackling.

Quilla I don't see the others. Hope this won't be a
flopperoonie.

Debit There's no such thing as a flopperoonie! Ah here
comes the Russian entry, Mr Artovsky from the
Soviet Union.

*Artovsky lumbers up and joins Debit and Quilla in the
dressing-room.*

Debit Welcome to the United Kingdom, Mr Artovsky.
You've met Quilla, I believe?

(Artovsky answers grudgingly.)

Artovsky I remember her.

(To Quilla.)

Beak still bent, comrade?

Quilla I'm going to eat you alive, you old hearthrug.

Debit Did you have a good trip, sir?

Artovsky It was a long, long march through the unending

snows. But I have strength, yes, I have
determination, yes, I have vodka, yes! And I am very
very glad to be here, but a little tired, yes, a little
tired ... .

*Artovsky begins to fall asleep as he does whenever
possible.*

Quilla   OK, we've got the American nation and the
hibernation. Let's get spangling!

Artovsky wakes up.

Debit   Here comes the British entry.

*(Rogan the lion, who is getting on, joins the other in
the dressing-room.)*

How was your journey Mr Rogan?

Rogan   Look, you know, I'm really meant to be King of the
Beasts, noamin? So it shouldn't be Mr Rogan it
should be King Rogan, right? Or you can call me
Your Menagerie.

Quilla   Did you have a good crawl?

Rogan   What? Oh. It was a real heavy number coming here.
Attacked by wild herds of beasts and humans.
Daring to venture where no lion has set paw before.
Battling for me life against super-leonine odds.

Artovsky   How far have you come, then?

Rogan   All the way from Finchley Central. That Northern
line's a battlefield, noamin?

Debit   Now there's just one more contestant to come.

Quilla   Only one more? I'll take on a hundred.

Artovsky   We have a legend in my country. All the animals
went to stay at the Hotel of the Beasts. There were a
thousand animals for breakfast. But at suppertime
there was only one bear.

Rogan   What???

Debit   Just one more contestant. The others were knocked
out in the early round. That leaves Quilla from
America, Artovsky from Russia, Rogan from Britain

and all we're waiting for is the winner of the African continent section. I don't know what's keeping her, but if she's not here in one minute precisely, she'll be disqualified. Are you all ready for the contest?

(Debit, Quilla, Rogan and Artovksy) *Song Contest Song*

Chorus
It's the Wild Animal Song Contest
It's going to be a wow
And how
It's the Wild Animal Song Contest
Buy your ticket now
With a roar and a caw and a bow wow wow
And a tweet and a hiss and a big miaow
We'll curse and worst and we'll cheer the
    best
In the Wild Animal Wild Animal Wild Animal
    Song Contest.

Quilla
I've got a song that's as wild as a stormy sky
It's a song with golden-feathered wonder-
    wings
I've got a song that'll teach you what it's like
    to fly
So just stand back and listen how a
    champion sings
And my song is bound to win number one
    position
In the cut-throat Animal Songsters
    Competition

Chorus
It's the Wild Animal Song Contest
(*Etc.*)

Artovsky
I've got a song that's as bright as the whitest
    snow
I've got a song that is warmer than a lionskin
    rug
I'll make you smile and I'm certain that your
    tears will flow
If you don't like it I'll give you a friendly hug
And my song is bound to win number one
    position

In the cut-throat Animal Songsters
Competition.

Chorus It's the Wild Animal Song Contest
(*Etc.*)

Rogan I've got a song that's as good as a juicy steak
And it's sung with silver throat and mighty
jaws
I've got a song that is guaranteed to make
you shake
You bet your life it's better than that song of
yours
And my song is bound to win number one
position
In the cut-throat Animal Songsters
Competition.

Chorus It's the Wild Animal Song Contest
It's going to be a wow
And how
It's the Wild Animal Song Contest
Buy your ticket now
With a roar and a caw and a bow wow wow
And a tweet and a hiss and a big miaow
We'll curse the worst and we'll cheer the best
In the Wild Animal Wild Animal

Debit We've no time for a mild animal

Chorus Wild Animal Wild Animal
Wild Animal
Song Contest!

Quilla Look, something's coming! Is it a tree?

Artovsky Is it a lamp-post?

Rogan Is it a drainpipe that's lost its house?

Debit No, it's the contender from Africa. Raffa the giraffe.

Quilla Good for a laugh.

Debit Oh yes.

*Raffa, a very weary female giraffe, drags herself up to
the others and gasps as they sing:*

(Debit, Quilla,
Rogan and Artovsky) *Making Fun of Raffa*

Debit Legs too long
Shoulders in a hunch
Your designer was
Out to lunch

Quilla Little black shoes
Long white socks
Built like a crane
At the London docks

All You don't need a sense of humour but you
have to laugh
At the dippy dopey dummy that they call
the giraffe.

Artovsky Buttoned up tight
In an old check coat
Hope you never catch
A bad sore throat

Rogan Ears in the clouds
Head in the air
Ever been asked
Is it cold up there?

All You don't need a sense of humour but you
have to laugh
At the dippy dopey dummy that they call the
giraffe.

Debit Raffa, you're from Africa?

Raffa Yes, a long way from Africa.

Debit Well, I suppose you wouldn't know, but over the
years we have built up certain traditions in the Wild
Animal Song Contest and one of those traditions is
puntuality.

Raffa Well, I got a puncture, mister.

Debit Not puncture – punctuality – being on time. And if
you can't fit in with our ways, you can always drop
out, you know. We do like to be efficient here, we

like animals to arrive on time, we like animals to sing on time, we like animals to sing in time, we like animals to sing in tune, oh you may think us fussy, you may think us quaint, and that's quite all right perhaps perhaps and then perhaps it ain't. What do you say to that?

Raffa I didn't hear all of it. Could you fetch a stepladder and say it again?

Rogan (*To Raffa.*) These contests sometimes get rough, noamin? Hope you don't mind a bit of aggro?

Quilla Shame you couldn't fly here, honey. You look totally wiped out.

Raffa Are you the Russian one?

Artovsky No, me, I am the Russian one. You know, giraffe person, you are not so suitably dressed for this contest. Could you not obtain some furs? It is more traditional for the animals to appear in furs.

Raffa I'm sorry.

Debit There's no such thing as sorry!

Raffa's Sorry Song

Raffa   Sorry
           I came a long long way
           Sorry
           I sometimes lost my way
           And I'm sorry
           Sorry sorry sorry
               Blue mountains of Africa
               I miss you
               Twisting trees of Africa
               I miss you
               Rich dark rivers of Africa
               Great brown plains of Africa
               Shadows of Africa
               I miss you
           Sorry
           I came a long long way
           Sorry

I sometimes lost my way
And I'm sorry
Sorry sorry sorry.

Debit   Very touching, I'm sure. But we've got to get on with rehearsals. First of all, I'll remind you of the rules. Rule One: each animal shall perform a song written by itself. Rule Two: each animal will be interviewed before performing and reply politely when asked about its hobbies and ambitions. Rule Three: political songs – about famine, unemployment or peace – are not to be sung. Rule Four: there must be no songs which make fun of human beings or penguins. Rule Five: for the contest itself, but not for rehearsals, the singers will perform wearing human being costumes and masks. This will add dignity to the proceedings. Rule Six: the winner will be awarded the title, King or Queen of the Animals and will be presented with the Million Gun plus one hundred thousand bullets for the Million Gun.

Raffa   What's the Million Gun?

The other animals laugh.

Debit   It's the gun which kills a million animals with every bullet. It's the greatest gun, and it's the only one. Now, we've just time to rehearse the show. I'll take Quilla in front of the cameras first. The rest of you – vanish yourselves and get ready.

(Debit takes his handmike and steps into the screen. Artovsky, Rogan and Raffa exit backstage. Bonzo takes his stand with a TV camera on his shoulder.)

I'm going to start the rehearsal now! Action! And now I'd like to introduce the unique, the amazing, the absolutely superfluous Inter-Galactic Universal Wild Animal Song Contest, coming to you live from … *(Insert name of venue.)*

I'm your loveable compere, my name's Kingsley Debit, and we're going to have fun, fun, fun and win the Million Gun! And here comes our first competitor. Will you please put your wings together for Quilla the Golden Eagle, representing the USA. Hello Quilla.

Quilla steps into the screen.

Quilla Well, Hi Mr Debit.

(*She pecks his cheek.*)

Been smoking kippers?

Debit Ha ha ha. Quilla, would you like to tell the animals out there in Viewerdom about your hobbies?

Quilla My hobby is winning. I always win.

Debit Well, isn't that nice? And what are you going to sing for us, Quilla?

Quilla It's a little hit I wrote called 'When the Eagle Smiles' and I'd like to perform it for you with my vocal backing group – The Bluebirds of Mayhem. Thank you, thank you very much.

Debit steps out of screen. Puppet Bluebirds perform aerobatics during choruses – their voices supplied by off-stage animals.

(Quilla and the Bluebirds of Mayhem)   *When the Eagle Smiles*

Quilla Now all you young animals gather round
Listen what the eagle is laying down
If you've got any sort of ears then you've
    certainly heard
That the Golden Eagle is the number one bird
And a wave of terror rolls for miles and miles
    When the eagle smiles.

Quilla and the Bluebirds Chorus And what is the eagle smiling about
As she rules the land and sea?
What is the eagle smiling about
She smiles because she's free
Free
Free.

Quilla	My claws are carved like crooked little spears My eyes of anger have never shed tears I stand on the mountain in my golden cloak Then I dive on my victim like a thunderstroke And a wave of terror rolls for miles and miles When the eagle smiles.
Quilla and the Bluebirds	And what is the eagle smiling about (*Etc.*)
Quilla	When I get em in my sights goodbye to hope The seal, the lamb and the antelope My beak is designed to rip and tear And that's what makes me Queen of the Air And a wave of terror rolls for miles and miles When the eagle smiles.
Quilla and the Bluebirds	And what is the eagle smiling about As she rules the land and sea? What is the eagle smiling about She smiles because she's free Free Free And you'd smile if you were me Don't you wish that you were Free like me?

Quilla comes off-screen into the dressing-room to be greeted by Debit.

Debit	Very nice, very nice.
Quilla	Very nice? It was great!
Debit	Well, it's a good song from an eagle's point of view. But not all the animals will go crazy for it.
Quilla	What can I do about that? You think I should make up a song about all the animals?
Debit	No, no be true to yourself and all that. It's a fine song, don't mess with it. What is really difficult, Quilla, is to win this contest.
Quilla	I'm gonna win. I always win.

Debit   I could make sure you won.

Quilla   I see. It's like that, is it?

Debit   It's always like that. You don't just win because you're the best. You win because the animal running the contest likes you best.

Quilla   So just what are you asking me for, honeyburger?

Debit   If you win the contest …

Quilla   Yeah?

Debit   You know an eagle is famous for being able to see a long way. And me. I just wish I had your vision.

Quilla   Penguins are short-sighted?

Debit   Right. And we can't fly very high up for one thing. I mean, a few flaps of these things is about all we can manage, fly a few feet, then splosh and we're back in the water. Course we can always trudge up to the top of an iceberg if there's one handy, but that takes time and we still can't see too far. So Quilla, when you win, after the presentation and all, we'll meet back here, and you can give me …

Quilla   What you want me to give you?

Debit   Your eyes.

Quilla   But I don't …

Debit   If you win the contest – you win the Million Gun and you'll be Queen over all the other animals. So you won't need your eyes so much, will you? Other animals will be proud to hunt for you. You could have a guide bird, a guide gull to lead you round the sky.

Quilla   I'll think about it, Debit.

Debit   If you want to win, you better think about it. Next, Artovsky!

Quilla leaves the dressing-room. Artovsky and Debit meet in the screen.

Debit   Now we'll make this a good rehearsal, won't we Mr Artovsky, and we'll try to stay wide awake, won't we? WON'T WE?

(*Artovsky blinks and nods.*)

And now, females and males of the specieses, the contesteroonie from the USSR! Do you have any ambitions, Mr Artovsky?

Artovsky   I would like to win this title King of the Animals and I would like to use my power to do some good in this poor old world of ours.

Debit   That's very nice, isn't it? And what are you going to sing for us?

Artovsky   I would like to sing, accompanied by my friends the Howling Wolves, a little number entitled 'The March of the Bear'.

Debit goes off-screen. Wolves appear – puppets or others – as backing group for Artovsky's first song.

The March of the Bear

Artovsky and Wolves

One two three four
I'm a bear of peace
And I march to war
Seven six five four three
Don't you wipe your feet on me

Three four one two
I'm going to bury you
Fours ones twos threes
I'm a fighting bear
And I'll kill for peace …

(He now speaks.)

Artovsky   No. It's crazy. I can't do it. That's the song they gave me to sing. But I don't like it. Don't believe in it. I'll sing a song I wrote myself. A song about my father.

The Dancing Bear

My father was a bear who danced
To a drummer's lively beat
All the people crowded round to see
My father stomp his feet

In the outposts of Siberia
Also at the Moscow fair

All the People stood with goggly eyes
To see a dancing bear

Was he a furry genius
Blessed with a dancer's brain
Oh no he was a frightened bear
And he danced out of pain

His master made him stand upon
A box of red-hot steel
Till when my father heard the drum
The painful heat he'd feel

And I am angry to my soul
About my father's fate
And that is why I do not dance
And that is why I hate.

Debit and Artovsky enter the dressing-room.

Debit   I'll give you some advice my friend. That second song was no good. Downbeat. Depressing. Do the first one.

Artovsky   But I didn't write the first one. It's cheating.

Debit   There's no such thing as cheating! Get in and win.

Artovsky   You think I can win? I don't know much about this mop music.

Debit   All you have to know is this – make the organiser happy.

Artovsky   And how can I make you happy, Mr Debit?

Debit   If you should win our contest, if you should win I would expect you to present me with your teeth and claws.

Artovsky   What?

Debit   Your teeth and claws, Mr Artovsky. If you win, I'll be under attack from the others. I'll have to defend myself. And how's a penguin meant to defend himself – with his flippers? No, I need weapons. If you win, you'll get the Million Gun. And I'll get teeth and claws.

Artovsky   Why you flat-footed waiter, I ought to …

Debit   Cool it, comrade. If you want to win, you know what to do. Next!

Artovsky goes and Rogan joins Debit in the screen.

Debit   And it's Rogan – United Kingdom! Got any hobbies, old man?

Rogan   Well, I used to collect, well, bones of dead animals, noamin?

Debit   And now you just collect fleas, right?

Rogan   Well, um ...

Debit   Ambitions?

Rogan   I'd like to have a number one hit record so I can make a lot of money and buy me mum a racehorse ...

Debit   For the Derby?

Rogan   No, for the dinner table. Anyway, my song is called 'Roarin'.'

Debit   Roarin' ...

Rogan   Right.

Debit leaves the screen. Rogan flexes his muscles before delivering his song.

Roaring Song

Rogan   You've seen me on golden syrup tins
             And movies by MGM
             I appeared with a witch and a wardrobe
             And I didn't think much of them
             I'm an artistocrat and a gentleman
             I never blow bubble gum
             And I talk real posh, for I never say gosh
             Or belly or blimey or bum
                  I go ROAR
                  That's right royal roaring
                  I go ROAR
                  It never gets boring
                  My ROAR
                  My wonderful ROAR
                  I go ROAR
                  I roar like a river
                  I go ROAR
                  And my enemies shiver

> At my ROAR
> My wonderful super-charged ROAR
> Now I had a job in a circus once
> And I didn't care much for that
> For they didn't treat me like a king
> But a musclebound pussy cat
> Now I'm not so young as I used to was
> But you'd better not forget
> Though my teeth are falling and my mane is
>   balding
> There's life in the old lion yet
>   I go ROAR
>   (*Etc.*)
> I used to go zebra-bashing
> Or take a little deer for lunch
> But now I'd rather be given a tin
> of Kit-e-Kat or Whiskas to munch
> But I haven't given up slaughtering
> I murder now and again
> I might bite in half some young giraffe
> And you'll know I'm still in business when
>   I go ROAR
>   That's right royal roaring
>   I go ROAR
>   It never gets boring
>   My ROAR
>   My wonderful ROAR
>   I go ROAR
>   I roar like a river
>   I go ROAR
>   And my enemies shiver
>   At my ROAR
>   My wonderful super-charged walloping
>   thatchery
>   ROOOOOOAAR!

Debit and Rogan meet in the dressing-room.

Debit You don't think you can win, do you?

Rogan Well ... you know, mate, it'll be the Yank or the Russian, won't it?

Debit   Could be. Or it could be you, Rogan.

Rogan   You like me song? Not bad, is it?

Debit   I like you, Rogan. I want you to win.

Rogan   That's funny. So do I.

Debit   I can make sure you win. But if I do, I'd like a little something in return.

Rogan   Right.

Debit   If you win, meet me afterwards, and give me your heart.

Rogan   Me heart?

Debit   You see, I'm not very brave. And I'd like to be brave. Being a coward is awful when you're facing hunters or cameras. So I need the heart of a lion. Debit the Lionheart. I'll get you fitted with a plastic hearteroonie.

Rogan   Thanks a lot, Debit. I'll give it a think or two. But it don't really seem fair.

Debit   There's no such thing as fair! Next! Raffa!

Raffa joins Debit in the screen. Rogan goes off.

Debit   And our last contestant tonight is Raffa from Africa. And Raffa is, as you can see, a giraffe. Have you any ambitions Raffa?

(Raffa stares hopelessly.)

Tiger got your tongue? Well, is there anything you want very much, Raffa?

Raffa   I want to go home.

Debit   Oh these amateurs! Just sing the song, sweetheart.

Raffa   It's called 'The Cameleopard.'

Raffa goes on screen. Debit goes off.

The Cameleopard

Raffa   There was a leopard
There was a leopard in the forest
His coat was the colour of the sun
There was a leopard

There was a leopard in the forest
Had a hundred black spots all different
There was a leopard
His eyes were sleepy flames
And he was lonely as a shooting star
As a shooting star

There was a camel
There was a camel in the desert
Her coat was the colour of the earth
There was a camel

There was a camel in the desert
She had a muddled mind but a perfect heart
There was a camel
Her eyes were shining coal
And she was lonely as an empty bird's nest
As an empty nest

Now the sun was walking down the sky one day
He squeezed a fat cloud till it had to rain
The rain collected up in a bowl of sand
Between the forest and the desert

And the leopard was thirsty
Colour of the sun
And the camel was dirty
Colour of the earth
So the leopard came to drink
And the camel came to bathe
In the deep cool of the pool

There was a leopard
There was a leopard in the forest
His coat was the colour of the sun
There was a camel
There was a camel in the desert
Her coat was the colour of the earth
And they met in the middle
Of the cool cool pool
And they stared at each other
Eyes of flame
Eyes of coal

And all their loneliness
Was burned and washed away
The giraffe is the child of their loving
The giraffe is the child of their love   } *(Repeat.)*

Debit leads Raffa to the dressing-room.

Debit   Pretty little song, Raffa, but you can't win.

Raffa   But I must win.

Debit   Why?

Raffa   If any of the other animals win that Million Gun, they'll use it to murder us all.

Debit   How do you know?

Raffa   I can read their eyes.

Debit   And what would you do with the Million Gun?

Raffa   I'd get rid of it. So there would be peace.

Debit   There's no such thing as peace.

Raffa   What do I have to do to win? What do you want?

What the Penguin Wants

Debit   The heart of the lion
                   I'm a coward in a fight
                   The eyes of the eagle
                   For I've very short sight
                   From the bear I want weapons
                   His teeth and his claws
                   But you're the giraffe
                   I want nothing of yours.

Raffa   I don't understand.

(Debit walks out.)

I don't understand at all. I've got a good song. I ought to win.

Bonzo stirs and emerges from under the dressing-room table where he has been concealed ever since the rehearsals started.

Bonzo   I'm Bonzo. The roadie. I like your song best.

Raffa Thanks, Bonzo.

Bonzo Message for you Raffa.

Bonzo hands over a piece of paper to Raffa. Bonzo runs off. Raffa reads the paper very slowly. While she reads, Debit herds Quilla, Artovsky and Rogan back into the dressing-room.

Debit Hurry up now, my furry and befeathered friends. Time to dress up in your human being costumes.

Debit flaps on out, leaving Quilla, Artovsky and Rogan to pull on bulky, baggy, ridiculous human being costumes of the sort that contestants wear in song contests. They complete the effect by donning 'human' masks which make them look totally ridiculous. (Basic kind of human masks, like the smiling face badge perhaps.) Raffa is still reading her note.

Raffa (*Without looking up.*) This is a serious thing, my friends.

She looks up, double-takes on the animals in human being costumes, opens her mouth wide, then begins to laugh and laugh and laugh. The other animals look at each other. They point at each other and begin to laugh too, till they are guffawing uncontrollably.

Quilla I'm not wearing this crazy outfit.

Artovsky But it's in the rules.

Rogan We'll have to change the rules, won't we?

They begin to take off their human costumes and masks.

Raffa Quilla.

Quilla What's the trouble, my spotty skyscraper?

Raffa You promised Debit to give him your eyes if you let him win.

Quilla It's not as simple as that …

Rogan What you mean, super-hooter?

Artovsky Stand back. I'll give you a demonstration of eagle-plucking.

(As they close in on Quilla.)

Rogan   Who's a pretty girl, then? You bent budgie!

Raffa   Artovsky?

Artovsky   *(Stopped in his tracks.)* Da?

Raffa   You said that if Debit let you win, you'd give him your claws and teeth.

Quilla   Why you nightmare version of Winnie-the-Pooh!

Rogan   You moth-eaten busby ...

Quilla   You fur-covered barrel ...

Rogan   Get your wellies on, Paddington, this is bear-bashing time.

Raffa   And you, Rogan.

Rogan   What's the matter, Babycham?

Raffa   You promised Debit your heart if he'd let you win.

Quilla   Why you overweight pussycat ...

Artovsky   You balding poodle ...

Quilla   Dandruff commercial ...

Artovsky   Dressing-gown tail ...

Rogan   Well, we all done it, didn't we? And we all got done, noamin?

Artovsky   All except Raffa ...

Quilla   All except Raffa. But what about Debit? That fish with flippers double-crossed the lot of us.

Artovsky   The whole contesteroonie is a lie. It is corrupt, it is no goodnik.

Rogan   It's a fiddle. It's an insult to my British sense of fair play.

Quilla   And my American sense of justice.

Artovsky   And my Russian sense of good jolly fun.

Quilla   Well, I don't want any part of the contest.

Artovsky   Nor me.

Rogan   Count me in for being counted out, noamin?

Raffa   But if we all drop out, that leaves Debit with the Million Gun.

Quilla	That's right. That's wrong.
Raffa	Debit would be King of the Beasts.
Artovsky	He'd wipe us all out.
Rogan	What can we do?
Raffa	We could join up together. We could be a group. Nobody could beat us then.
Quilla	Raffa, that's a great idea. We'll be a group. I'll sing lead, you guys be my backing group and we'll do a little number I wrote about laying eggs …
Artovsky	Wait a moment, ladybird. I'll sing my songsky, you sing alongsky …
Rogan	Hangabahtabit. I got a little song …
Raffa	But a group can't just be a one-man show, or a one-woman show for that matter.

(Raffa, Quilla, Artovsky, Rogan)   *Group a Group*

Raffa	If you want to grow a forest It takes more than a single tree You need more than a bucket of water If you want to start a sea Takes more than salt and pepper If you're cooking lentil soup Takes more than a voice and a pretty face To make a group a group …
Quilla	They may have been the very best of all But there's more to the Beatles than John or Paul
Artovsky	And I don't care what anyone thinks Took more than Ray Davies to make the Kinks
Rogan	And the thunder and lightning of Zeppelin aren't The unassisted work of Robert Plant
Raffa	The sound of the Stones can make you stagger But it wouldn't work if it was just Bill Wyman
Quilla	A good voice needs a good band behind Like the Pretenders with Chrissie Hynde
Artovsky	And a voice on its own is just no use

	Ask Edwyn Collins of Orange Juice
Rogan	David Sylvian of Japan
Raffa	Andy Taylor of Duran Duran
Quilla	Phil Oakey of Human League, they'll all agree
Artovsky	Plus Terry Hall of Fun Boy Three
Raffa	Boy George of Culture Club he won't quibble
	Nor will the Damned's Captain Sensible
Quilla	Cheryl Baker of Bucks Fizz
Artovsky	Clare Grogan of Altered Images
Rogan	Buster Bloodvessel, David Van Day
	Know that working as a group is the only way
Quilla	The Thompson Twins, U2 and the Clash
	Know that working solo is the way to crash
Artovsky	And Suggs of Madness knows for a fact
	There's always something missing in a solo act

Rogan, David Sylvian of Japan

Raffa, Andy Taylor of Duran Duran

Quilla, Phil Oakey of Human League, they'll all agree

Artovsky, Plus Terry Hall of Fun Boy Three

Raffa, Boy George of Culture Club he won't quibble
Nor will the Damned's Captain Sensible

Quilla, Cheryl Baker of Bucks Fizz

Artovsky, Clare Grogan of Altered Images

Rogan, Buster Bloodvessel, David Van Day
Know that working as a group is the only way

Quilla, The Thompson Twins, U2 and the Clash
Know that working solo is the way to crash

Artovsky, And Suggs of Madness knows for a fact
There's always something missing in a solo act

(With Quilla, Artovsky and Rogan singing backing vocals.)

Raffa, So if you want to fly the Concorde
It takes more than a one-man crew
You need more than a couple of gerbils
If you want to start a zoo
Takes more than salt and pepper
If you're cooking chicken soup

Quilla, Takes more than a gimmick

Artovsky, And a jacket that glows

Rogan, And a synthesiser

Raffa, And a cute little nose

Takes a song that goes flying
Higher than trees
Building up chords
And magic harmonies
Takes a gang of mates
That can loop the loop
Takes more than a voice and a pretty face
To make a group a group a group
To make a group a group

Quilla	Hey, we're a group!
Artovsky	Feels good in the belly. Beats fighting.
Rogan	It's all right, init? Working together.
Raffa	We've got to work out some more songs, who plays what, taking turns to sing lead and all that.
	Debit enters in human mask and military officer's costume – dress uniform, not camouflage.
Debit	What's up? What's up? Why aren't you in your human costumes?
Raffa	We're not wearing that stuff, Debit. We're animals and we're proud to be animals.
Quilla	And we're a group now.
Artovsky	We're all going to sing together …
Rogan	In harmony …
Debit	No, no, you can't do that. Nothing good will come of that. You can't all win. You've got to compete. You've got to fight each other. That's the way progress gets made.

The Land of War

Debit
You can't get nothing by loving
You can't get nothing through chat
Don't waste time in discussion
There's no percentage in that
Go in and grab it
Go out and nab it
That's what your right arm's for
Without competing
You won't be eating
Marching through the Land of War
Fight for your kids
Fight for your wife
Fight for your King and Country
Fight for your life
Might is right
Force is the law
That's how we do it

In the Land of War
Now when you're climbing the ladder
There's other people below
Place your boots upon their fingers
Until the blighters let go
Up to the top now
Don't ever stop now
What if the blood should pour?
Shout alleluia
Do them before they do yer
Marching through the Land of War
>Fight for your kids
>Fight for your wife
>Fight for your King and Country
>Fight for your life
>Might is right
>Force is the law
>That's how we do it
>In the Land of War.

Debit And that, my lords, ladies, gentlemen and others, is my wonderful entry for the Wild Animal Song Contest.

Raffa (*To audience.*) Well, what do you think of Debit's performance so far?

Audience Rubbish!

Raffa Well, Rogan's written a song haven't you?

Rogan Yeah. It might teach Debit a thing or two. But it's not all that good, mind.

Raffa I bet it's a smasheroonie. Come on, Rogan.

Rogan, Quilla, Artovsky and Raffa step into the screen. Debit listens.

(Rogan, Quilla, Artovsky, Raffa)

Rogan

New Lion

Lion was a bully
Lion pushed around
All the small animals
Lion found

Lion was a killer
Lion hunted down
All the tall animals
Lion found

(With Quilla, Artovsky and Raffa.)

Rogan   And he gloried in his courage
And his fighting skill
And he gloried in his muscles
And he gloried in the kill
Yes he gloried in the kill

But the corpses of his victims
They began to stink
And the lion he sickened
And the lion began to think
Yes the lion began to think

And the power of his thoughts
Was wonderful and strange
And with every golden thought
Came a golden change

Rogan   Now lion is a lover
Lion's having fun
Rolling round on his back
In the sun

Lion is a lover
What you think of that?
Loves to purr like a great
Golden Cat

(With Quilla, Artovsky and Raffa.)

Rogan   And he glories in all creatures
And he delights to play
And dance and sing with others
Every peaceful golden day
Every peaceful golden day.

Quilla   Artovsky's got something to announce.

Artovsky   Un, well during that song, Quilla here asked me if I'd marry her. And I say Da!

Quilla   That means yes.

Artovsky   Let's tell the world about it, baboushka.

Quilla   Da!

Artovsky   Yea yeah yeahsky!

(Quilla and Artovsky)   *The Wedding of the Eagle and the Bear*

Quilla
USSR and USA
They got married
On a marigold day

Artovsky
USA and USSR
They drove past the moon
In a silverside car

Quilla and Artovsky
Now the whole world knows
They were deadliest foes
Tearing at each other's throats
Till they dumped their money
Took a dozen combs of honey
And sailed around the skies in a pea-green boat

Quilla
USA and USSR
Settled down upon
A Saturday star

Artovsky
USSR and USA
Had two children
Called Oh and Kay

Quilla
Kay and Oh got bigger one day
They packed their rockets
And zooted away

Artovsky
And if you ask me where they are
I suppose they've flown
To the Milky Bar

Quilla
And if you ask me where they stay
I couldn't know less
But I guess they're OK

Quilla and Artovsky
Now where eagles dare
To be wed to the bear

The world takes a holiday
For you need no money
And there's tons and tons of honey
At the marriage of the USSR
To the USA.

Raffa   OK friends, let's explain to poor old Debit how a group works.

Quilla   It's cooperation …

Artovsky   It's teamwork …

Rogan   It's taking turns, noamin?

During the next song, Debit gets out of his human costume and mask.

(Quilla, Artovsky, Rogan, Raffa)   *Take your Turn*

Quilla   You jump out
Sing your song
Might get it right
Might get it wrong
You jump out
Jump back
It didn't take long

All   But the beat keeps going
Yes it moves along
The beat keeps going
When your bit's done
Oh the beat keeps going
So hang on tight
Cos the beat is sweet
And the beat is right
And it rocks all day
And it rocks all night

Artovsky   You take turns
Bear alive
Make with a shake
Give em that jive
You take turns
Do your act

	That's all A natural fact
All	But the beat keeps going
	(*Etc.*)
Rogan	You walk out Do your worst Bop till you pop Bop till you burst You walk out Face your fate Walk back Wasn't that great?
All	But the beat keeps going
	(*Etc.*)
Raffa	You step out Make your move Loon to the tune Grind to the groove You step out Take your chance Time's up Everyone dance
All	But the beat keeps going
	(*Etc.*)

(*Debit is now out of human costume and mask.*)

Debit   That's all very well. But you've broken all the rules. You refused to wear your human being costumes. And you wouldn't compete against each other. You're all out of the contest, you're all disqualified.

Quilla   Why don't you waddle off and lay an egg?

Rogan   On your bike, Debit.

Debit   We must have the prize-giving. Animalesses and Animals, because all the contestants have broken the rules of the Wild Animal Song Contest, you will be delighted to hear that the organiser of the contest, myself, will accept the prize for my own song, The Land of War, which you loved so much.

(*Bonzo appears carrying the amazing looking Million Gun. He stands in front of Debit.*)

I have great pleasure in accepting, on behalf of myself, the title of King of the Beasts, along with the famous Million Gun. As you know, the Million Gun can kill one million animals with each bullet. It is a great honour – careful Bonzo.

(*Bonzo is pointing the Million Gun at Debit.*)

Bonzo   Sit down and listen. It's my turn at last.

Bonzo's Rap

(*Spoken over music.*)

Bonzo   I may be old
But my nose is cold
I'm hearty and I'm hale
And my ears stick up
Like a six-month pup
And there's plenty of wag in my tail

And I've worked for an age
At my job backstage
And they never caught me napping
But now the old tyke
Gets his chance at the mike
So dig what this old dog's rapping

I may be old
But my nose is cold
I'm hearty and I'm hale
And my ears stick up
Like a six-month pup
And there's plenty of wag in my tail

I've carried mikes and amps
And speakers and lamps
But I've never been unhappy
Cos I like the load
Of a life on the road
And they pay me in Pal and Chappie

Yeah I may be old
But my nose is cold
I'm hearty and I'm hale
And my ears stick up
Like a six-month pup
And there's plenty of wag in my tail.

Bonzo You have it, Raffa.

Bonzo hands over the Million Gun to Raffa. She examines it, then carefully takes a piece off it, as if it might explode.

Raffa We'll take it to pieces.

Quilla What'll we do with the pieces?

Bonzo Put them in the Peace Maker.

Bonzo proffers a large receptacle – maybe based on a tea urn. Raffa drops her piece in. Each animal takes turns in gingerly removing another piece until all pieces are placed in the machine.

Raffa Blow cold.

(*All blow instruments.*)

Blow hot.

(*All blow again.*)

Blow with everything you've got.

All blow an almighty chord. The tap of the tea urn is turned by Raffa. From the tap flows a golden liquid into a can held by Bonzo. This is poured into a third container, which has two compartments. Some steam rises – or coloured smoke. Raffa carefully takes out of the third container a wonderful golden elephant. The Million Gun has been transformed into an elephant. Note: The Peace Maker can be a very simple or a marvellously Heath Robinson machine depending upon resources.

Debit What's the elephant in aid of?

Raffa Elephants for peace.

Debit How's that?

Rogan   Strong and gentle, mate. Strong and gentle.
             (*Debit is half-crying.*)

Debit   I don't know what to do.

Raffa   Don't worry. The world's much safer now there's no
             such thing as a Million Gun.

Debit   What I mean is, you all looked so happy when you
             were singing together. And I felt so lonely when I
             sang on my own. Everybody else is in a group. And I
             haven't got a group to be in – wah wah wah ...
             Debit bawls.

Raffa   Would you like to join our group?

Debit   Could I?

Raffa   You'll have to ask the group.

Debit   Please can I join the group?

Quilla   OK.

Artovsky Welcome, Debit, my brother.
             *Artovsky hugs Debit – a little too much. Debit squeaks
             and is freed.*

Rogan   Mind, you'll have to take turns, noamin?

Debit   Da. I mean yes.

Raffa   Peace – yes! War – no!

             Everything's going to be all right. Let's go!

**(Rogan, Raffa,
Artovsky, Quilla,
Debit, Bonzo
and Audience)**   *Peace*

Rogan   Lions for peace
                   Physical and mental
                   Prove you're strong
                   By acting gentle

Raffa   Giraffes for peace
                   In our wild hot home

Artovsky   Bears for peace
                   And the honeycomb

Quilla   Eagles for peace

	And clean blue air
	No bombs or rockets
	Anywhere
Debit	Penguins for peace
	On them open seas
Bonzo	Dogs for peace
	And a lot more trees
Rogan	Lions for peace
All	Peace for lions
Raffa	Giraffes for peace
All	Peace for giraffes
Artovsky	Bears for peace
All	Peace for bears
Quilla	Eagles for peace
All	Peace for eagles
Debit	Penguins for peace
All	Peace for penguins
Bonzo	Dogs for peace
All	Peace for dogs
All	Women for peace – Peace for women
	Men for peace – Peace for men
	Children for peace – Peace for children
	The world for peace – Peace for the world

The end.

Mowgli's Jungle

Adrian Mitchell

LIST OF CHARACTERS

Herdswoman
Shere Khan | A tiger
Mowgli (The Little Frog) | A boy raised by wolves
Mother Wolf
Father Wolf
Tabaqui | A jackal
Akela
The Fat One
Wild Sister | All wolves
Grey Wolf
Baloo | A bear
Bagheera | The black panther
Kaa | The python
Chil | The kite
The Bandar-log tribe | Monkeys
Cobra
Ikki | The porcupine
Messua | A middle-aged woman
1st Villager
2nd Villager
Buldeo | A boastful hunter
Priest
Mr Barnstaple | Forest Officer
Daisy Barnstaple | His daughter

SCENES

Act One

Act Two

MOWGLI'S JUNGLE

Act One

Scene One: A Death at Dawn

The Jungle. A blue stream. Sounds of the Jungle at dawn. A herdswoman talks to her baby son.

Herdswoman   Way back! This is where the great Jungle begins. And, once it begins, the Jungle goes on forever. You help me herd these cattle, little one. Go on, you help me, it's an easy task. Yes, herding cattle is one of the laziest things in the world. The cattle move and crunch, and lie down, and move on again, and they do not even low. They only grunt, and the buffaloes very seldom say anything. Those buffaloes get down into the muddy pools one after another, and they work their way into the mud till only their noses and staring china-blue eyes show above the surface. And they lie there like logs. The sun makes the rocks dance in the heat.

And then you hear one kite, just one and never any more, one kite whistling almost out of sight over your head. And you know that if one of the cowherds dies, or a cow dies, that kite will sweep down, and the next kite miles away will see him drop and follow, and the next, and the next, and almost before they are dead, there'll be a score of hungry kites come out of nowhere.

When you're a big boy you'll herd the cattle with the other children. You'll sleep and wake and sleep again, and weave little baskets of dried grass and put grasshoppers in them. Or you'll catch praying mantises and make them fight. Or you'll string a necklace of red and black jungle-nuts; or watch a lizard basking on a rock, or a snake hunting a frog near the wallows. And you'll sing long, long songs and the day will seem longer than most people's lives. And perhaps you'll make a mud castle with mud figures of men and horses and buffaloes, and put reeds into men's hands, and pretend that they are kings with armies or that they are gods to be worshipped.

Then evening will come, and you'll make your call. And the buffaloes will lumber up out of the sticky mud with noises like gunshots going off one after the other … my little son, my little son. Almost time to feed you. But first, let me drink.

Shere Khan, an enormous tiger with a limp, begins to emerge from the Jungle. He stalks the woman. At the last moment she hears it, rolls over, rises to a crouch and confronts the tiger. Without taking her gaze off it, she pushes the baby so that it falls into the entrance of a small cave – the entrance to a wolf's lair. She rises and turns to run.

Scene Two: The Little Frog

A cave. A small cave with a small, round entrance.

Mother Wolf is lying on her side, feeding her four baby wolves.

Father Wolf stands over the wrapped baby, which lies on the floor of the cave.

Sound of the baby crying quietly. Father Wolf sniffs the baby thoroughly.

Mother Wolf   What is that thing?

Father Wolf   A man's cub! It is alive!

Sounds of a baby gurgling, laughing up at Father Wolf.

Mother Wolf   Is that a man's cub? I have never seen one. Bring it here.

Father Wolf picks up the baby in his jaws and puts it beside the feeding wolf-cubs.

Mother Wolf   How little! How soft!

(*She pushes the baby in among her cubs.*)

And – how bold! Ah – he is taking his meal with the others. And so, this is a man's cub. Now, was there ever a wolf that could boast of a man's cub among her children?

Father Wolf   I have heard now and again of such a thing, but never in our Pack or in my time. He is altogether without hair, and I could kill him with a touch of my foot. But see, he looks up and is not afraid. Somebody comes, hide him.

Mother Wolf turns so as to hide her cubs and the baby.

Mother Wolf   Who is it?

Father Wolf   A jackal.

Tabaqui, the jackal, appears in the entrance of the cave.

Tabaqui   Not just a jackal – it is Tabaqui, the Dish-Licker.

Father Wolf   What do you seek, Tabaqui?

Tabaqui   Good luck go with you, O wondrous wolf, and good luck and strong white teeth go with the noble children, that they may never forget the hungry in this world.

Mother Wolf   Tabaqui, you are a maker of mischief, a teller of tales and an eater of rags.

Tabaqui   That is true, Mother Wolf, that is all too true. But you will not refuse me the scraps of your lair? I know you despise me, and I surely deserve your scorn. But I have powerful friends in the Jungle, do I not?

The roar of Shere Khan is heard in the distance. Father Wolf speaks stiffly.

Father Wolf   Enter, then, and look for yourself. But there is no food here.

Tabaqui	For a wolf, no. But for so mean a person as myself a dry bone is a good feast. Who am I, the humble Tabaqui, the mangey dish-licker to pick and choose? There is a strange smell . . .

Father Wolf takes a bone from a pile and throws it before Tabaqui.

Father Wolf	A bone for you.

Tabaqui sniffs it and licks his lips.

Tabaqui	All thanks for this good meal. Ah, how beautiful your noble children are!
Mother Wolf	You must know, Tabaqui, that there is nothing so unlucky as to praise children to their faces.
Tabaqui	My apologies, have I made mischief again. Well, let me tell you some news. Shere Khan, the great tiger, has shifted his hunting-grounds. He will hunt among these hills for the next moon, so he has told me.

Father Wolf looks angry.

Father Wolf	He has no right! By the Law of the Jungle he has no right to change his hunting-ground without due warning. He will frighten every animal within ten miles, and I – I have to kill for two, these days.

Mother Wolf speaks quietly.

Mother Wolf	His Mother did not call him Lungri, the Lame One, for nothing. He has been lame from his birth. That is why he has only killed cattle. Now the villagers are angry with him. They will scour the Jungle for him and we and our children must run when the grass is alight. Indeed, we are very grateful to Shere Khan!
Tabaqui	Shall I tell him of your gratitude?
Father Wolf	Out! Out and hunt with thy master. You have done enough for one day.

Tabaqui speaks quietly.

Tabaqui	I go. You can hear Shere Khan below in the thickets, I might have saved myself the message.

(He stops just before he leaves.)

There is a strange smell here, a very strange smell.

Tabaqui exits. A dry, angry sing-song whine is heard.

Father Wolf Shere Khan! He is a fool – that cry will frighten away all the cattle and deer in the valley.

Mother Wolf Hush! It is neither cattle nor deer he hunts tonight. It is man.

Father Wolf The Law of the Jungle forbids it. Kill one man and a hundred arrive with guns and gongs and rockets and torches. Then everybody in the Jungle suffers.

Suddenly the head of Shere Khan appears in the entrance to the cave. The voice of Tabaqui is heard behind him.

Tabaqui My lord, my lord it went in here!

Father Wolf speaks politely but angrily.

Father Wolf Shere Khan does us great honour. We would invite him in were the entrance to our lair large enough to admit him. What does Shere Khan desire?

Shere Khan My quarry. A man's cub is here. The cub has no mother. Give it to me.

Father Wolf The wolves are a free people. They take orders from the Head of the Pack, and not from any stupid cattle-killer. The man's cub is ours – to kill if we choose.

Shere Khan You choose and you do not choose! What talk is this of choosing? Am I to stand nosing into your dog's den for my fair dues? It is I, Shere Khan, who speak.

Mother Wolf shakes herself clear of her cubs and the baby and springs forward as Shere Khan roams. She confronts him.

Mother Wolf And it is I, Raksha the Demon, who answer. The man's cub is mine, Shere Khan, mine. He shall not be killed. He shall live to run with the Pack and to hunt with the Pack. And in the end, you hunter of little naked cubs, you frog-eater, you fish-killer – he shall hunt you. Now go, or you will leave my lair lower than ever.

Shere Khan backs away from Mother Wolf's fury.

Shere Khan   Each dog barks in his own yard! We will see what the Pack will say to this fostering of man-cubs. The man's cub is mine, and to my teeth he shall come in the end, Oh bush-tailed robbers.

Shere Khan backs away. Mother Wolf throws herself down with her cubs.

Father Wolf   Shere Khan speaks this much truth. The cub must be shown to the Pack. Will you still keep him, Raksha?

Mother Wolf   Keep him? He came to us alone and hungry and helpless; yet he was not afraid. Look, he has pushed one of my babies to one side already. And that lame butcher would have killed him and run off while the villagers hunted through all our lairs in revenge! Keep him? Yes I will. Lie still little frog. O Mowgli – for I will call you Mowgli the Frog – the time will come when you will hunt Shere Khan as he has hunted you.

Father Wolf   But what will the Pack say?

Scene Three: The Pack Decides

The Council Rock. A large rock dominates a small clearing. Moonlight. Wolves assemble in a circle. They include Mother Wolf (with wrapped baby) and Father Wolf. Also Akela, the ageing chief in the pack, Baloo the bear and Grey Wolf, a young and eager wolf who becomes Mowgli's brother. Akela leads the pack in howling – wolves howl in harmony to give the impression that there are far more of them than you think – and in the night-song of the Jungle, the wolves sing.

Wolves   Now Chil the Kite brings home the night
That Mang the Bat sets free –
The herds are shut in byre and hut,
For loosed till dawn are we.

This is the hour of pride and power,
Talon and tush and claw.
Oh, hear the call! Good hunting all
That keeps the Jungle law!

When the sun flares, get to your lairs
Behind the breathing grass:
For cracking through the young bamboo
The warning whispers pass.
By day made strange the woods we range
With blinking eyes we scan:
While down the skies the wild duck cries:
'The day – the day to man'!

But when the kite brings home the night
That Mang the Bat sets free –
The herds are shut in byre and hut,
For loosed till dawn are we.
This is the hour of pride and power,
Talon and tush and claw.
Oh, hear the call! – Good hunting all
That keeps the Jungle Law!

Akela	Let the Pack be silent! The Council is met. It is the full moon and it is the time for the Pack to inspect its new cubs. Those that are accepted are free to run where they please.
Wild Sister	Akela, our Leader, I ask that my cub be accepted.
Akela	You know the Law – you know the Law. Look well, O Wolves!
Other Wolves	Look well, O Wolves!
	The other wolves sniff the cub and murmur together. There is silence.
Akela	Is it well with the cub?
Other Wolves	It is well.
Akela	Then the cub is ours. We must guard her and teach her.
Other Wolves	The cub is ours.
Mother Wolf	Akela, our Leader, I ask that the man-cub, Mowgli the Frog, may be accepted.

Akela   You know the Law – you know the Law. Look well, O Wolves!

Shere Khan appears.

Shere Khan   Mine Mine Mine
The Man-cub is Mine
Mine Mine Mine
The cub is Mine.
Give him to me. What have the Free People to do with a man's cub?

Akela   Look well, O Wolves! What have the Free People to do with the orders of any save the Free People? Look well!

Wild Sister   What have the Free People to do with a man's cub? I dispute the right of the man's cub to join the Pack.

Akela   It is your right. Then two members of the Pack who are not the father and mother must speak for the cub. Who speaks for the cub? Among the Free People, who speaks?

Baloo   The man's cub – the man's cub? I speak for the man's cub. There is no harm in a man's cub. I have no gift of words, but I speak the truth. Let him run with the Pack, and be entered with the others. I myself will teach him.

Akela   We need another voice. Baloo has spoken, and he is our teacher for the young cubs. Who speaks besides Baloo?

Bagheera   O Akela, and you the Free People. I have no right in your assembly, but the Law of the Jungle says that the life of a rejected cub may be bought at a price. And the Law does not say who may or may not pay that price. Am I right?

The Wolves speak hungrily.

Wolves   Good! Good! You are right Bagheera. Listen to the great black panther. The cub can be bought for a price. It is the Law.

Bagheera   Knowing that I have no right to speak here, I ask your leave.

Wolves   Speak then.

Bagheera   To kill a naked cub is shameful. Besides, he may make better sport for you when he is grown. Baloo has spoken on his behalf. Now to Baloo's word I will add one bull. A fat bull, newly killed, not half a mile from here. This bull is yours if you accept the man's cub according to the Law. Is it difficult?

Wild Sister   What matter? He will die in the winter rains. He will scorch in the sun. What harm can a naked frog do us?

Grey Wolf   Let him run with the Pack.

Father Wolf   Where is the bull, Bagheera?

Grey Wolf   Let him be accepted.

Akela   Look well – look well, O Wolves. Is it well with the Man-cub?

Wolves   It is well.

Akela   Then the Man-cub is ours.

Wolves   The Man-cub is ours.

Shere Khan   Mine Mine
The Man-cub will be Mine
Mine Mine
The Man-cub will be MINE!

Bagheera   Aye, roar well, for the time comes when this little creature will make you roar another tune, or I know nothing of man.

The wolves begin to disperse. Akela comes down from his rock and joins Bagheera.

Akela   It was well done. Men and their cubs are very wise. He may be a help to us one day.

(He speaks to Father and Mother Wolf.)

Take him away. Train him as one of the Free People.

Akela and Bagheera are now left alone.

Bagheera   Truly Akela, he may be a help in a time of need. For no one can hope to lead the Pack for ever.

Akela   You make the truth sound soft, Bagheera. You mean this – that there comes a time to every leader of every pack when his strength goes from him and he becomes feebler and feebler, till at last he is killed by the younger wolves and a new leader is chosen – to be killed in his turn.

Bagheera   It is a hard truth. But perhaps Mowgli the Frog may soften it for you.

Akela   Perhaps. If he lives and if he learns.

Bagheera   He will learn. I know the ways of men. He will learn.

Scene Four: Mowgli Learns the Jungle

Baloo and Bagheera, the latter reclining on a branch, the former scratching, are waiting. After a moment, the Young Mowgli leaps in and does a few cartwheels, then lies down and strokes Bagheera's head.
Bagheera purrs loudly.

Baloo   Come along Mowgli. Time for lessons.

Young Mowgli   Must we? Bagheera?

Bagheera   Must we? Yes, we must.

Young Mowgli stands up and stretches, then puts his hands behind his back and faces Baloo.

Baloo   Repeat the Hunting Verse.

Young Mowgli repeats a lesson.

Young Mowgli   Feet that make no noise; eyes that can see in the dark; ears that can hear the winds in their lairs, and sharp white teeth, all these things are the marks of our brothers except Tabaqui the Jackal and the Hyena whom we hate.

Baloo   Wood and Water Laws: how do you tell a rotten branch from a sound one?

Young Mowgli   By its shape and by its colour and by its shaking.

Baloo   What should you do before splashing into a pool?

Young Mowgli   I should warn the water-snakes below me.

Baloo   What must you do when you hunt outside your own hunting-grounds?

Young Mowgli   I must repeat aloud the Stranger's Hunting Call.

Baloo   Repeat it.

Mowgli repeats the Call.

Young Mowgli   Give me leave to hunt here because I am hungry.

Baloo   And what is the answer to the Call?

Young Mowgli   If you eat any more you'll be fat as Baloo.

Baloo swipes angrily at Young Mowgli with his paw.

Baloo   No! It is: hunt then for food, but not for pleasure.

Young Mowgli yells at being hit, and runs off into the Jungle.

Bagheera   Have a care, Baloo.

Baloo   'There is none like to me', says the cub in the pride of his earliest kill. But the Jungle is large and the cub he is small, let him think and be still. That is one of my laws, Bagheera. A Man-cub must learn all the Law of the Jungle.

Bagheera   But think how small he is. How can his little head carry all your long talk?

Baloo   Is there anything in the Jungle too little to be killed? No. But I only smacked him very softly.

Bagheera   Softly! What do you know of softness, old Iron Feet? You've bruised his face with your softness.

Baloo   I am now teaching him the Master-words that shall protect him, if he will only remember the words, from all in the Jungle. Is that not worth a little bruise?

Bagheera   Well, see that you do not kill the Man-cub. He is not a tree-trunk to sharpen your blunt claws upon. But what are those Master-words?

Baloo   I will call Mowgli and he shall say them – if he will. Come, Little Brother!

Mowgli looks sullen.

Young Mowgli   My head is ringing like a bee-tree. I came for Bagheera and not for you, fat old Baloo!

Baloo	That is all one to me. Tell Bagheera, then, the Master-words of the Jungle that I have taught you.
Young Mowgli	Master-words for which people? The Jungle has many tongues. I know them all.
Baloo	You know a little, Man-cub, but not much. See, Bagheera, they never thank their teacher. Say the word for the Hunting-People then, great scholar.
	Mowgli speaks with a bear-like accent.
Young Mowgli	We be of one blood, you and I.
Baloo	Good. And now the Master-word for the birds.
	Mowgli speaks in a high voice with a kite whistle at the end.
Young Mowgli	We be of one blood, you and I.
Bagheera	And the word for the Snake-People?
	Mowgli gives a wonderful long hissing sound which so delights him that he applauds himself and jumps astride Bagheera's back.
Baloo	There, not so bad!
	(Baloo speaks to Bagheera.)
	I begged the Master-words from Hathi the wild Elephant. And Hathi took Mowgli down to a pool to get the Snake-word from a water-snake, because I could not pronounce it. And now Mowgli is fairly safe from accidents in the Jungle, for neither snake, bird or beast will hurt him.
Bagheera	But Shere Khan, the lame one, has sworn to kill him. And there is his own tribe, too.
Young Mowgli	But I shall have a tribe of my own, and lead them through the branches all day long.
Bagheera	What is this new folly, little dreamer of dreams?
Young Mowgli	Yes, and we shall throw branches and dirt at old Baloo, they have promised me this. – Ah!
Baloo	Mowgli, you have been talking with the Bandar-log – the Monkey-People.
Bagheera	You've been with the Monkey-People – the grey

apes – the people without a Law – the eaters of
everything? That is shameful.

Young Mowgli   When Baloo hurt my head I went away, and the grey
apes came from the trees and had pity on me. No
one else cared.

Baloo   The pity of the Monkey-People! The stillness of the
mountain stream! The cool of the summer sun! And
then, Man-cub?

Young Mowgli   And then, and then they gave me nuts and pleasant
things to eat, and said I was their blood-brother
except that I had no tail and that I should be their
leader one day.

*Two monkeys appear behind Baloo and Bagheera
and copy their actions mockingly.*

Bagheera   They have no leader! They lie. They have always lied.

Young Mowgli   They were very kind and asked me to come again.
Why have I never been taken among the Monkey-
People? They can use their hands as I do.

(Baloo grabs hold of Mowgli and sits on him.)

They do not hit me with hard paws. Let me get up!
Bad Baloo, let me up! I want to play with them again.

Baloo   Listen, Man-cub, I have taught you all the Law of the
Jungle – for all the peoples of the Jungle – except
the Monkey-Folk who live in the trees. They have no
Law. They are outcasts. They have no speech of
their own, but use the stolen words which they
overhear. We of the Jungle have no dealings with
them. We do not drink when the monkeys drink, we
do not hunt when the monkeys hunt, we do not die
where they die. Have you ever heard me speak of
the Bandar-log till this day?

*Young Mowgli manages to stifle his laughter at the
monkeys, who continue to mock Bagheera and Baloo
behind their backs.*

Young Mowgli   No. Baloo.

Baloo   The Jungle-People put them out of their mouths and
out of their minds. They are very many, evil, dirty,

shameless and they want to be noticed by the
Jungle-People. But we do not notice them even when
they throw nuts and filth on our heads.

*Immediately, a shower of nuts and dirt descends on
Baloo's head.*

Baloo The Monkey-People are forbidden. Forbidden to the
Jungle-People. Remember.

Baloo allows Young Mowgli to stand up.

Bagheera You Baloo should have warned Young Mowgli
against these clowns.

Baloo How was I to guess that he would play with such
dirt? The Monkey-People!

Bagheera Let us remind him of the Law of the Jungle, Baloo.

Baloo With pleasure, Bagheera.

*Baloo and Bagheera sing sometimes singly sometimes
together, while Young Mowgli and the two monkeys
perform spectacular acrobatics behind them.*

Baloo and Now this is the Law of the Jungle – as old and as true
Bagheera as the sky;

And the wolf that shall keep it may prosper, but the
wolf that shall break it must die.

As the creeper that girdles the tree-trunk the law
runneth forward and back –

For the strength of the pack is the wolf, and the
strength of the wolf is the pack.

Wash daily from nose-tip to tail-tip; drink deeply, but
never too deep;

And remember the night is for hunting, and forget
not the day is for sleep.

The jackal may follow the tiger, but cub, when thy
whiskers are grown,

Remember the wolf is a hunter – go forth and get
food of thine own.

The kill of the wolf is the meat of the wolf. He may
do what he will,

But, till he has given permission, the pack may not eat of that kill.

Because of his age and his cunning, because of his gripe and his paw,

In all that the law leaveth open, the word of the head wolf is law.

Now these are the Laws of the Jungle, and many and mighty are they:

But the head and the hoof of the law and the haunch and the hump is – obey!

Baloo and Bagheera turn to where Young Mowgli should be applauding – but he has disappeared with the monkeys. Baloo and Bagheera look astonished and then they look up and see Young Mowgli and the monkeys vanishing through the trees.

Bagheera   Bring him back! Bring him back!

Baloo   My best pupil! My only pupil! Stolen away by the Bandar-log!

Bagheera   Why did you not warn the Man-cub? What was the use of half-killing him with blows if you didn't warn him?

Baloo   Let's hurry – we may catch them yet.

Bagheera   How can we? The Monkey-People have their own woods and cross roads through the trees, they travel like a hurricane. We must make a plan.

Baloo   Arrula! Whoo! They may have dropped him already, being tired of carrying him. Who can trust the Bandar-log? Put dead bats on my head! Give me black bones to eat! Roll me into hives of the wild bees that I may be stung to death, and bury me with the Hyena, for I am the most miserable of bears! Arrulala! Wahooa! Oh, Mowgli, Mowgli! Why did I not warn thee against the Monkey-Folk instead of breaking your head? Now perhaps I may have knocked the day's lesson out of his mind, and he will be alone in the Jungle without the Master-Words.

Bagheera   He gave me all the Words correctly a little time ago.
Baloo you have neither memory nor respect. What
would the Jungle think if I, the Black Panther, curled
myself up like Ikki the Porcupine and howled?

Baloo   What do I care what the Jungle thinks? He may be
dead by now.

Bagheera   Unless and until they drop him from the branches in
sport, or kill him out of idleness, I have no fear for
the Man-cub. He is wise and well-taught, and above
all he has the eyes that stare and make the Jungle-
People afraid. But he is in the power of the Bandar-
log, and they, because they live in trees, have no
fear of any of our people.

An idea occurs to Baloo.

Baloo   Fool that I am! Oh, fat brown, root-digging fool that I
am! It is true what Hathi the Wild Elephant says: 'To
each his own fear'.

Bagheera   How does this saying help us?

Baloo   The Bandar-log fear Kaa the Rock Python. He can
climb as well as they can. He steals young monkeys
in the night. The whisper of his name makes their
wicked tails turn cold. Let us go to Kaa.

Bagheera   What will a snake do for us? He is not of our tribe,
being footless – and with most evil eyes.

Baloo speaks hopefully.

Baloo   He is very old and very cunning. Above all, he is
always hungry. Promise him many goats to eat.

Bagheera   He sleeps for a full month after he has eaten. He may
be asleep now, and even were he awake what if he
would rather kill his own goats?

Baloo   You and I will persuade him, old hunter. There lies
Kaa, let's go and wake him. Kaa! Kaa!

*(Kaa is seen, a great rock python with a big, blunt-
nosed head. He is twisting his thirty-foot body into
curves and knots and licking his lips.)*

He has not eaten. Be careful, Bagheera! He is always

a little blind after he has changed his skin, and very quick to strike. Good hunting, Kaa!

Kaa   Good hunting for us all? Oho, Baloo, what are you doing here? Good hunting, Bagheera!

Bagheera Good hunting Kaa!

Kaa   One of us at least needs food. Is there any news of game? A doe now, or even a young buck? I am as empty as a dried well.

Baloo speaks casually.

Baloo   We are hunting.

Kaa   Give me permission to come with you. A blow more or less is nothing to you, Bagheera or Baloo, but I – I have to wait and wait for days in a wood-path and climb half a night on the mere chance of a young ape. Pss-haw! The branches are not what they were when I was young. Rotten twigs and dry boughs.

Baloo   May be your great weight has something to do with the matter.

Kaa   I am a fair length. But for all that, it is the fault of this new-grown timber. I came very near to falling on my last hunt – very near indeed – and the noise of my slipping, for my tail was not tight-wrapped round the tree, waked the Bandar-log, and they called me most evil names.

Bagheera speaks as if trying to remember something.

Bagheera Footless, yellow earth-worm was it?

Kaa   Sssss! Have they ever called me that?

Baloo   It – it is the Bandar-log that we follow now.

Kaa   It can be no small thing that takes two such hunters – leaders in their own Jungle – on the trail of the Bandar-log.

Baloo   Indeed. I am no more than the old and sometimes very foolish Teacher of the Law to a Wolf Pack, and Bagheera here . . .

Bagheera snaps his jaws.

Bagheera . . . is Bagheera. The trouble is this Kaa. Those nut-stealers and pickers of palm-leaves have stolen away our Man-cub, of whom you have perhaps heard.

Kaa I have heard some news from Ikki the Porcupine, of a man-thing that was entered into a wolf-pack, but I did not believe it. Ikki is full of stories half heard and very badly told.

Baloo But it is true. He is such a Man-cub as never was. The best and wisest and boldest of Man-cubs – my own pupil, who shall make the name of Baloo famous through all the jungles. And besides, I – we – love him, Kaa.

Kaa shakes his head to and fro.

Kaa Tss! Tss! I also have known what love is. There are tales I could tell you that . . .

Bagheera But our Man-cub is in the hands of the Bandar-log now, and we know that of all the Jungle-People they fear Kaa alone.

Kaa They fear me alone? They have good reason. They called me 'yellow fish' was it not?

Bagheera Worm – worm – earth-worm, as well as other things which I cannot now say for shame.

Kaa We must remind them to speak well of their master. Aaa-ssh! Where did they go?

Baloo The Jungle alone knows. Toward the sunset, I believe.

Chil the kite appears high over their heads, crying.

Chil Up, up, up, up, Hillo! Illo! Illo! Look up, Baloo, look up! It is I, Chil the Kite.

The animals look up and see the kite.

Baloo What is it?

Chil I have seen Mowgli being carried away by the Bandar-log. He told me to mark his trail and tell you. I watched. The Bandar-log have taken Mowgli the Frog beyond the river to the monkey city – the Cold Lairs. They may stay there for a night or ten nights, or only an hour. I have told the bats to watch

through the dark-time. That is my message. Good
hunting, all you below!

Bagheera   A full stomach and a deep sleep to you, Chil. I will
remember you in my next kill, and put aside the
head for you alone, O best of kites!

Chil   It is nothing. The boy held the Master-word. I could
do no less.

Chil flies off.

Baloo   He has not forgotten to use his tongue. To think of
one so young remembering the Master-word for the
birds too while he was being pulled across trees!

Bagheera   It was most firmly driven into him. But I am proud of
him and now we must go to the Cold Lairs.

Baloo   I have never been there.

Bagheera   It was once a city of men. But no men have lived
there for a thousand years. We can be there in half a
night's journey – at full speed.

Kaa   Let us travel fast.

Bagheera   We dare not wait for you, Baloo. You follow us, we
must go ahead – Kaa and I.

Kaa   They called me speckled frog.

Bagheera   Worm – earth-worm. Yellow earth-worm.

Kaa   Let us go on.

Baloo   I will go as fast as I can.

Baloo, Bagheera and Kaa exit.

Scene Five: The Cold Lairs

*The Jungle and the ruined city which is occupied by
the Bandar-log. The Monkeys swing Young Mowgli
along through the Jungle, singing as they move.*

Monkeys   Here we go in a flung festoon
Half-way up to the jealous moon!

Don't you envy our pranceful bands?
Don't you wish you had extra hands?
Wouldn't you like if your tails were – so –
Curved in the shape of a Cupid's bow?
Now you're angry, but – never mind.
Brother, thy tail hangs down behind!

All the talk we ever have heard
Uttered by bat or beast or bird –
Hide or fin or scale or feather –
Jabber it quickly and all together!
Excellent! Wonderful! Once again!
Now we are talking just like men.
Let's pretend we are … never mind,
Brother thy tail hangs down behind!
This is the way of the monkey-kind.

Then join our leaping lines that scumfish through
     the pines,
That rocket by where, light and high, the wild-grape
     swings.
By the rubbish in our wake, and the noble noise we
     make,
Be sure, be sure, we're going to do some splendid
     things!

The Monkeys pull bits of foliage back to reveal a great throne. They persuade Young Mowgli, who is half afraid and half excited, to go towards it.

1st Monkey Mowgli the Frog! Welcome to the Cold Lairs!

Monkeys Mowgli the Frog! Welcome to the Cold Lairs!

1st Monkey You are Mowgli the Frog! We are the Bandar-log!

Monkeys You are Mowgli the Frog! We are the Bandar-log!

By now Young Mowgli is seated on the throne.

1st Monkey There is no one in the Jungle so wise and good and clever and strong as the Bandar-log.

Monkeys There is no one in the Jungle so wise and good and clever and strong as the Bandar-log.

1st Monkey Oh wonderful, wonderful Monkey-people, hark to my fine speaking. Mowgli has come to be our

	wonderful, wonderful King.
Monkeys	Wonderful, wonderful King.
Young Mowgli	I wish to eat. I am a stranger in this part of the Jungle. Bring me food, or give me leave to hunt here.
1st Monkey	You shall not hunt, oh mighty Mowgli! I will send many monkeys to fetch you nuts and wild pawpaws.
Young Mowgli	Are you sure they will remember?
1st Monkey	You jest, Oh King. For we are great.
Monkeys	We are great.
1st Monkey	We are free.
Monkeys	We are free.
1st Monkey	We are the most wonderful people in the Jungle.
Monkeys	We all say so and it must be true.

The 1st Monkey takes a shining crown from under the throne to crown Young Mowgli.

1st Monkey	And now I crown the mighty Mowgli and now he is the King.
Monkeys	Now he is the King.
1st Monkey	Oh King, reign for ever, or until we become tired of you.
Monkeys	Until we become tired of you.
Young Mowgli	I am no King.
1st Monkey	To us you are a King. We need a King. Kings are most amusing.
Monkeys	Most amusing.
1st Monkey	So let us amuse you with a little song.

During the song that follows, the Monkeys dance around Young Mowgli's throne. At first they throw flower petals and bow to him, but gradually the song and dance becomes more and more sinister. During the last verse, a tall white cobra rises from the floor in front of Young Mowgli's throne so that he cannot leave the throne. The Monkeys dance as they sing.

Monkeys	Ere Mor the peacock flutters, ere the Monkey-People cry,

Ere Chil the kite swoops down a furlong sheer,
Through the Jungle very softly flits a shadow and a
    sigh –
He is fear, O little hunter, he is fear!
Very softly down the glade runs a waiting, watching
    shade,
And the whisper spreads and widens far and near;
And the sweat is on thy brow, for he passes even
    now –
He is fear, O little hunter, he is fear!

1st Monkey   Now you are a powerful King, you must take a
powerful bodyguard. Arise, O great white cobra!

Monkeys   When the heat-cloud sucks the tempest, when the
    slivered pine-trees fall,
When the blinding, blaring rain-squalls lash and
    veer;
Through the war-gongs of the thunder rings a voice
    more loud than all –
It is fear, O little hunter, it is fear!
Now the spates are banked and deep; now the
    footless boulders leap –
Now the lightning shows each littlest leaf-rib clear –
But thy throat is shut and dried, and thy heart
    against thy side
Hammers: fear, O little hunter – this is fear!

Cobra   Small Stranger, where is the King?

Young Mowgli   What King?

Cobra   The great King of the City of Twenty Kings. The great
city of the forest whose gates are guarded by the
King's towers. Who are you, sitting down before me,
knowing not the name of the great King?

Young Mowgli   Mowgli they call me. I am of the Jungle. The wolves
are my people. Father of Cobras, who are you?

Cobra   I am the guardian of the King's Treasure. Kurran Raja
sent me here to guard his treasures in the days
when my skin was dark, that I might teach death to
those who came to steal. Where is the King?

Young Mowgli	There is no King.
Cobra	Some brave men have found their way here. But I found them. And they cried only a little time. And now you come and put on the great King's crown and sit on the great King's throne. By the Gods of the Sun and Moon you will die if you attempt to leave that throne.

The Cobra and Young Mowgli face each other and freeze.

The Monkeys begin to chant and clap their hands and sway as the Cobra sways and Mowgli's head begins to nod. Suddenly Bagheera and Baloo and Kaa, leap into the clearing.

Kaa	Do not fear, Mowgli the Frog. Hold out your hand to the white Cobra.
Young Mowgli	Baloo! Can I trust this great rock python?
Baloo	Trust him with your life.

Mowgli reaches out his hand. The Cobra does not strike.

Kaa	He is so old that his poison fangs are withered black and all dried up.
Young Mowgli	Why, Cobra, you are nothing but a white, white worm.
Kaa	I don't think you should say that.
Bagheera	Let's take the Man-cub and go.

Mowgli and his friends battle against the Monkeys. The Monkeys are driven back and finally frozen by the hypnotic powers of Kaa.

Bagheera	They may attack again.
Kaa	They will not move until I order them. Stay you sso!
Bagheera	Baloo, are you hurt?
Baloo	I think they've pulled me into a hundred little pieces. Wow! I am sore. How is the Man-cub?
Young Mowgli	I am sore, hungry and bruised. But very happy.
Bagheera	It is to Kaa that you owe your life. Thank him

according to our customs, Mowgli.

Kaa   So this is the Manling. Very soft is his skin, and he is not so unlike the Bandar-log. Have a care, Manling, that I do not mistake you for a monkey some twilight when I have changed my coat.

ACT TWO

Scene Six: The Leadership

The Council Rock, early evening. Ikki the porcupine enters and settles down. Three wolves – Wild Sister, Grey Brother and The Fat One enter playfully. They stop and stare. Shere Khan speaks from off-stage.

Shere Khan   Good hunting to you.

Wolves   Good hunting, Shere Khan.

Shere Khan enters, followed by the smiling jackal, Tabaqui.

The Fat One   Good hunting, Tabaqui.

The other wolves find it hard to conceal their disgust at the jackal.

Tabaqui   Good, good hunting to you, Oh sleek ones. It has been good hunting I hope?

Grey Brother   It is always good hunting with the Pack.

Wild Sister   Grey Brother speaks only for himself. For myself I could eat a crocodile and a cobra.

The Fat One   Nuts and berries, that was my dinner. Nuts and berries. I am the greedy one and I like to feast on torn red flesh and crunching bones.

Shere Khan   Indeed, the Jungle is a hard world. Accept the gift of a few remains.

Shere Khan pushes some bones with his foot towards the wolves.

Grey Brother   What is it?

Tabaqui laughs.

Tabaqui   It was a fine red deer – until an hour ago. And then the mighty Shere Khan leaped upon its back, and his claws tore at the hide of the deer until it was striped and striped like a tiger, only that the stripes were red and spurting red . . .

Shere Khan	Enough, Tabaqui, it was an ordinary kill. There was nothing brave about it. But how is it that such strong young wolves as yourselves go hungry? There is plenty of prey.
Grey Brother	Our luck is out.
	Wild Sister laughs.
Wild Sister	What loyalty! Our luck is out! No, Grey Brother, our leadership is out.
The Fat One	We have two leaders. Two. There is Akela and there is Mowgli the Frog.
Grey Brother	And Akela is wise and Mowgli is endlessly cunning.
Wild Sister	And Akela is an old and feeble wolf. And Mowgli is no wolf. He is a Man-cub. We should not trust him.
	Shere Khan sighs.
Shere Khan	Yes, it has always been a wonder to me.
Grey Brother	What makes you wonder?
Shere Khan	That such a pack of strong and clever and agile wolves should accept the leadership of a dying wolf. And that such a pack should worship the Man-cub.
Grey Brother	We do not worship Mowgli, but he is of the Pack.
Shere Khan	Oh, I heard he was become a God. I heard that at the Council you dare not look him between the eyes.
Wild Sister	It is true what you hear. And it is shameful to the Pack.
Grey Brother	Come! It is the Pack's business. And no business of yours, Shere Khan.
	The wolves exit. The Fat One speaks as he is leaving.
The Fat One	Thank you for the shin-bone, Shere Khan!
	Shere Khan turns to Tabaqui. They are beside Ikki but pay no heed to him.
Shere Khan	Tabaqui, I feel that it is time to strike.
Tabaqui	Good. You must punish Grey Brother. His insolence is not to be borne, O my Master.
Shere Khan	Dish-Licker, Rat-Catcher, Terror of the Spiders –

listen to me. Let Grey Brother go his way. But keep your red eyes fixed upon the Man-cub. For before the moon changes, I will drink the blood from his throat and tear the heart from his chest.

Exit Shere Khan and Tabaqui. Enter Bagheera. Ikki the Porcupine spreads his pines – Bagheera goes over to him.

Bagheera   Good hunting, Ikki. Whisper to me about your latest adventures, O spikey one.

(Bagheera puts her head down by Ikki and listens. We hear whispering noises. Bagheera startled, jumps and pricks his ear on the spines. He licks his paw to wipe his ear.)

Oww! Shere Khan will drink the blood from his throat and tear the heart from his chest. Ikki, I think you have saved the Man-cub's life. I would kiss you but – hmm! Let me offer you a mango instead.

(Bagheera sticks a fruit on a spine of Ikki's. Exit Ikki, snuffling.)

Mowgli! Mowgli!

Mowgli swings in on a vine and climbs higher up it.

Mowgli   Ah, Bagheera! You are looking beautiful and black today.

Bagheera   Come down, Little Brother, come down. I have a secret for you. Little Brother, how often have I told you that Shere Khan is your enemy?

Mowgli   What of it? Shere Khan is all long tail and loud talk.

Bagheera   Shere Khan dare not kill you while the Pack protects you. But many of the younger wolves believe what Shere Khan has taught them – that a Man-cub has no place with the Pack.

Mowgli   I was born in the Jungle, I have obeyed the Law of the Jungle and there is no wolf of ours from whose paws my clever hands have not picked thorns. Surely they are still my brothers.

Bagheera   Little Brother, feel under my jaw. There is no one in

the Jungle that knows that I, Bagheera, carry that
mark – the mark of the collar. And yet, Little Brother,
I was born among men, and it was among men that
my mother died – in the cages of the King's Palace
at Oodeypore. And because I had learned the ways
of men, I became more terrible in the Jungle than
Shere Khan. Is it not so?

Mowgli Yes. But why should my brothers and sisters turn
against me?

*Mowgli stares at Bagheera. After a moment, the
panther turns his head away.*

Bagheera That is why. Not even I can look you between the
eyes, and I was born among men, and I love you,
Little Brother. The others – they hate you because
their eyes cannot meet yours – because you are
wise – because you have pulled out those thorns
from their feet – because you are a man.

Mowgli frowns.

Mowgli I did not know these things.

Bagheera What is the Law of the Jungle, Mowgli? Strike first
and then speak. When Akela misses his next kill –
the Pack will turn against him and against you. They
will hold a Jungle Council at the Rock and then – and
then – I have it! Go down quickly to the man's huts in
the valley, and take some of the Red Flower which
they grow there, so that when the time comes you
may have even a stronger friend than I or Baloo or
those of the Pack that love you. Get the Red Flower.

Mowgli The Red Flower? That grows outside their huts as
darkness falls? I will get some.

Bagheera There speaks the Man's cub. Remember that it
grows in little pots. Get one swiftly, and keep it by
you for time of need.

Mowgli Good! I go. But are you sure, O my Bagheera, that all
this is Shere Khan's doing?

Bagheera I am sure, Little Brother.

Mowgli Then, by the bull that bought me, I will pay Shere

Khan in full for this, and perhaps a little more. I go to hunt among the ploughed fields of Man!

Mowgli rushes off. Bagheera is left alone.

Bagheera That is a man. That is all a man. O Shere Khan, never was a blacker hunting than that frog-hunt of yours ten years ago.

(*The wolves howl.*)

What's that?

Baying is heard off-stage.

Akela enters. The wolves speak from off-stage.

Wolves Akela! Akela! Let the lone Wolf show his strength. Room for the Leader of the Pack! Spring, Akela.

Akela Do not say, Good Hunting, Bagheera. My hunting days are done.

Scene Seven: Stealing the Red Flower

A hut in the village. A bed is the only furniture. A wicker basket, plastered with earth inside, contains burning charcoal and sticks. The basket has a handle. Messua, a middle-aged Indian woman, is preparing some food in the hut. Mowgli approaches and sees the fire.

Mowgli There it is, the red flower!

Mowgli melts back into the Jungle as Messua comes out of the hut with a small pot of food. She sings.

Messua My husband was strong
My husband was warm
His loving was
A thunderstorm
But a fever came
And took him by the hand
Now he is dancing,
Dancing, dancing

With the ghosts in ghostland.
My baby could stand
My baby could dance
His hands and legs
Like little plants
But a tiger came
And took him by the hand
Now he is dancing,
Dancing, dancing
With the ghosts in ghostland.

She takes sticks and feeds the fire.

Mowgli   I understand. The red flower is like me. It will die
unless it is given things to eat.

Messua continues singing.

Messua   And now I am poor
As poor as a stone
All day and night
Alone alone
Let dreams tonight
Take me by the hand
And I'll go dancing,
Dancing, dancing
With the ghosts
With my lovely ghosts
With my lovely ghosts in ghostland.

*Messua goes back into the hut. Mowgli picks up the
fire pot.*

Mowgli   Come with me, Red Flower. I will feed you well and
care for you.

*Exit Mowgli. Messua comes out of the hut with a
spoon. She sees the fire has gone and screams.*

Scene Eight: Mowgli's Farewell

*The Council Rock. Akela lies beside the rock, not on it.
Shere Khan sits beside Tabaqui, Wild Sister and The Fat*

One. Bagheera, Baloo and Grey Brother sit together.

Shere Khan And so Akela has missed his kill. Now he must lie beside the Council Rock as a sign that the leadership of the Pack is open. And now we call him the Dead Wolf, for that is what we call a Leader of the Pack who has missed his kill. He is the Dead Wolf for as long as he lives, which will not be long.

Bagheera You have no right to speak. You would not have dared when Akela was in his prime.

Shere Khan According to the Law, the Dead Wolf should be killed . . .

Baloo No, for Mowgli is not here.

Shere Khan What has a Man-cub to do with wolves?

Mowgli appears with the fire pot and a branch in his hands.

Mowgli What has a tiger to do with our leadership? Free People – does Shere Khan lead the Pack?

Shere Khan The leadership is open and I was asked to speak.

Mowgli By whom? Have Wild Sister and The Fat One changed so much to praise Shere Khan? The leadership of the Pack is with the Pack alone.

The Fat One Silence.

Wild Sister Man-cub!

Grey Brother Let him speak! He has kept our Law.

Mowgli Let Akela speak.

Wolves Aye. Let the Dead Wolf speak.

Akela speaks wearily.

Akela Free People, and you too, followers of Shere Khan. For a long time I have led you to and from the kill, and in all my time not one has been trapped or maimed. Now I have missed my kill. You know how that plot was made. You know how you brought me up to an untried buck to make my weariness known. It was cleverly done. Your right is to kill me here on the Council Rock, now. Therefore, I ask, who comes to kill the Dead Wolf? For it is my right, by the Law of the Jungle, that you come one by one.

There is a pause. Nobody wants to fight Akela alone.

Shere Khan   Bah! What have we to do with this toothless fool? He is doomed to die! It is the Man-cub who has lived too long. Free People, he was my meat from the first. Mine. Give him to me.

Wild Sister   Let him go to his own place.

Shere Khan   And turn all the people of the village against us? No, give him to me. He is a man, and none of us can look him between the eyes.

Akela   He has eaten our food. He has slept alongside us. He has hunted for us. He has broken no word of the Law of the Jungle.

Bagheera speaks gently.

Bagheera   Also, I paid for him with a bull when he was accepted. The worth of a bull is little, but perhaps Bagheera's honour is something that he will fight for.

The Fat One   A bull paid ten years ago! What do we care for ten-year old bones?

Bagheera   And what do you care for a promise? Well are you called the Free People!

Shere Khan howls.

Shere Khan   No man's cub can run with the People of the Jungle. Give him to me!

Akela   He is our brother in everything but blood, and you would kill him here! In truth, I have lived too long. Some of you are eaters of cattle, and of others. I have heard that, under Shere Khan's teaching, you snatch children at night from the villager's door-step. Therefore I know you are cowards, and it is to cowards that I speak. It is certain that I must die, and my life is of no worth, or I would offer that in the Man-cub's place. But I promise that if you let the Man-cub go to the village, I will die without fighting.

Shere Khan's Party   He is a man! A man! A man!

Bagheera speaks to Mowgli.

Bagheera   Now the business is in your hands.

Baloo   I'm afraid we'll have to fight.

Mowgli   Listen, you! There is no need for this jabbering. You have told me often that I am a man so I, the man, have brought here a little of the Red Flower which you fear.

Mowgli thrusts the branch into the fire pot, and brings it out flaming. The wolves cower away. Bagheera speaks to Mowgli.

Bagheera   You are the Master. Save Akela from death. He was ever your friend.

Mowgli looks around staring.

Mowgli   Good! I go from you to my own people – if they be my own people. The Jungle is shut to me, and I must forget your talk and your companionship. But there is a debt to pay before I go.

(Followed by Bagheera, Mowgli strides over to Shere Khan and catches him by the tuft on his chin.)

Up dog! Up, when a man speaks, or I will set that coat ablaze.

(Shere Khan gets up.)

This cattle-killer said he would kill me.

(Mowgli beats Shere Khan with a flaming branch.)

Thus and thus, then do we beat dogs when we are men. Stir a whisker, Lame One, and I ram the Red Flower down your throat. Pah! Singed jungle-cat, go now! But remember when next I come to the Council Rock, it will be with Shere Khan's hide on my head.

(Shere Khan exits followed by Tabaqui.)

For the rest, Akela goes free to live as he pleases. You will <u>not</u> kill him, because that is not my will. Nor do I think that you will sit here any longer, lolling out your tongues as though you were somebodies, instead of dogs whom I drive out – thus! Go!

He drives away The Fat One and Wild Sister. Mowgli looks around. He is left with his allies.

Bagheera   Here comes your father and your mother to say farewell.

Father Wolf and Mother Wolf come to Mowgli. He puts his arms round them. He weeps.

Mowgli   What is it? What is it? I do not wish to leave the Jungle, and I do not know what this is. Am I dying Bagheera?

Bagheera   No, Little Brother. Those are only tears such as men use. Now I know that you are a man, and a man's cub no longer. The Jungle is shut to you from now on. Let them fall, Mowgli. They are only tears.

Mowgli   Now I will go to men. You will not forget me?

Baloo   Never, never.

Grey Brother   Never while I can follow a trail. Come to the foot of the hill when you are a man and I will talk with you. I will come near to the village and play with you at night.

Father Wolf   Come soon! Oh, wise Little Frog, come again soon; for we are old, your Mother and I.

Mother Wolf   Come soon, little son of mine; for listen, child of man, I loved you more than ever I loved my cubs.

Mowgli   I will surely come. And when I come it will be to lay out Shere Khan's hide upon the Council Rock. Do not forget me! Tell them in the Jungle never to forget me.

Mowgli begins, slowly, to walk away from the Jungle. Those who remain, sing.

Baloo,
Bagheera
and Wolves   When the heat-cloud sucks the
tempest, when the slivered pine-trees fall,
When the blinding, blaring rain-squalls lash and
          veer;
Through the war-gongs of the thunder rings a voice
          more loud than all –
It is fear, O little hunter, it is fear!

Now the spates are banked and deep; now the
    footless boulders leap -
Now the lightning shows each little leaf-rib clear -
But thy throat is shut and dried, and thy heart
    against thy side
Hammers: fear, O little hunter - this is fear!

Scene Nine: Mowgli and the People

A hut (as in Scene Seven) and a village clearing.

*Buldeo, a boastful hunter, is seated on the ground
stringing a bow. Messua is cooking. The 1st Villager is
showing the 2nd Villager a tin trunk.*

1st Villager I bought it from the batman of a Scottish officer.

2nd Villager It is a very fine trunk.

1st Villager But it was expensive. He charged me.

2nd Villager Oh, that's terrible.

1st Villager But it's full of wonderful clothes.

2nd Villager What kind of clothes?

*(The 1st Villager opens the trunk and takes out a pair
of tweed knickerbockers, Scottish clothes.)*

Oh dear.

*The 1st Villager, angry, slams the trunk. Dogs barking.
Mowgli comes jogging in. He stops and spreads his
hands in greeting. The Villagers, Buldeo and Messua
stare.*

1st Villager What is it?

2nd Villager Don't touch it. It may be a forest spirit. I'll fetch the
Priest.

The 2nd Villager runs off-stage.

Messua He is a handsome boy. He has eyes like red fire. He is
like my boy that was taken by the tiger.

Buldeo He's a savage.

1st Villager	Is the great hunter afraid of him?

The Villagers keep staring as Mowgli speaks.

Mowgli	They have no manners, these Men-Folk. They jabber and point and stare. Only the grey ape would behave as they do.
Buldeo	I'm not afraid of a boy just because he's a savage.
1st Villager	Or an evil spirit, perhaps.
Buldeo	We'll see if he's a spirit.

(Buldeo pinches Mowgli. Mowgli yells, then retreats from Buldeo, biting the back of his own hand. Buldeo advances and pinches Mowgli again, then turns away.)

He's real enough.

(Mowgli bites Buldeo's bum. Buldeo leaps into the air.)

Arre! The demon has bitten me. I've got rabies!

The 2nd Villager returns with a Priest, a portly man dressed in white with a red and yellow mark on his forehead.

2nd Villager	And he might have horns hidden under that hair.
Priest	Calm yourselves.

Buldeo takes out a knife.

Buldeo	He's a mad dog.

Buldeo runs at Mowgli who smiles and trips him deftly. Buldeo gets to his feet again and is about to stab Mowgli who is looking at his knife with interest when the Priest holds back his hand.

Priest	Gently, Buldeo, gently. Let me examine the creature.

(The Priest stares at Mowgli.)

He is nothing to be afraid of. Look at the white scars all over his arms and legs. They are the bites of wolves.

Buldeo	Wolf bites, yes those are certainly wolf bites.
Priest	He is only a wolf-child run away from the Jungle. Hmm! This will interest the Sahib.

(The Priest now speaks to the 2nd Villager.)

	Fetch Mr Barnstaple, the Forest Officer.
2nd Villager	But his house is five miles away, on top of the hill.
Priest	This afternoon the Forest Officer and his daughter are taking tea at my house. Run and invite them here to see this wonder.

The 2nd Villager speaks wildly as he runs.

2nd Villager	Mr Barnstaple, Mr Barnstaple.
Buldeo	He's vicious. He bit me on the leg.

The 1st Villager looks down the back of Buldeo's clothes.

1st Villager	Oh dear, it's turning purple and green.

Buldeo jumps. The Priest is still examining Mowgli. Mowgli speaks from the side.

Mowgli	By the bull that bought me, but all this talking and fuss is like another looking-over and sniffing-over by the Pack! Well, if I am a man, a man I must become.

Mr Barnstaple, an English Forest Officer in tropical gear, enters with his daughter Daisy, a beautiful young English girl.

Barnstaple	All right, where's this wonder, then?
Priest	Mr Barnstaple – may I present a fine example of a wild boy.
Daisy	How wild is he?
Barnstaple	That's enough, Daisy.
Priest	Apparently he was brought up in the Jungle by wolves.
Barnstaple	I have heard such stories before from the last Forest Officer, but . . .
Priest	He has the little scars of wolf bites on his legs and arms.
Barnstaple	And he's been living in my Jungle has he? Can he talk?
Priest	I don't know.

Barnstaple goes up to Mowgli.

Barnstaple	Can you talk?
	Mowgli points into his own mouth.
Daisy	I think he's hungry, papa.
Barnstaple	Oh well. Er, have him fed. And teach him to talk.
Priest	What language shall we teach him?
Barnstaple	English of course. When he can hold a reasonable conversation, send him along to me.
Buldeo	But he bit me, Sahib. He bit me on the back.
Barnstaple	Buldeo, have you ever thought where we would be without pain?
	Buldeo looks confused.
Buldeo	No, Sahib.
Barnstaple	Well, think about it.
	(Barnstaple starts to exit but then sees the tin trunk.)
	What's in there?
	(He opens the lid.)
	Oh, Scottish clothes.
	He slams the lid and exits. Daisy waves to Mowgli.
Daisy	Goodbye wild boy.
	Daisy exits. Mowgli makes an attempt to return her wave but doesn't know the gesture. Then he patiently points at his open mouth again and shows it to people.
Priest	And now he must be fed. Who will look after the wild boy – feed him, give him a place to sleep and teach him English?
1st Villager	My husband is not well.
2nd Villager	My English is very bad.
Buldeo	I'd rather give house-room to a cobra.
Messua	He is like the boy that was taken. I will look after him.
	The Priest looks upwards.
Priest	What the Jungle has taken, the Jungle has restored. The poorest woman in the village, a widow without relations left alive, will bring up the savage. Take the

boy into your house my sister, and forget not to honour the Priest who sees so far into the lives of men.

Messua finds a coin and gives it to the Priest. The Villagers move away and exit as Messua takes Mowgli by the hand. As Buldeo leaves, Mowgli filches his knife from his belt and hides it. Messua leads Mowgli towards the hut.

Mowgli speaks from the side of the stage.

Mowgli   A trap. She's trying to get me into a trap.

He moves back. Messua walks into the hut without him to show him it's alright and comes out again, twice. He takes her hand and follows her in.

Messua   Food first. Food.

(She gives him a little bowl of steaming rice. Mowgli puts it on the ground and sniffs it. He smiles at Messua and begins to lick the rice. Messua takes a second bowl and starts eating the rice with her fingers.)

Food. Food.

(Mowgli tries to eat it with fingers but finds it funny.)

Food.

Mowgli   Foo.

Messua   Foo_d_. Foo_d_.

Mowgli   Fooder. Fooder.

Messua   Yes, good, good.

(Messua points to herself.)

Messua. Messua.

Mowgli   Fooder.

Messua   Not Fooder. Messua, Messua.

Mowgli   Mefyore. Mefyore.

Messua   Messua.

Mowgli   Messua.

(Mowgli suddenly points to himself.)

Mowgli. Mowgli.

He looks very pleased with himself.

Messua Mow-gli. Mowgli.

Mowgli dances around, chanting.

Mowgli Mowgli, Mowgli, Mowgli.

He stops suddenly and Messua points to him again.

Messua Mowgli – Wild Boy.

Mowgli Mowgli Wileboy. Mowgli Wileboy.

He resumes his dance, whirling around the hut. He comes to a stop beside a little picture stuck on the wall. He fetches Messua who points her finger at the picture.

Messua Queen Victoria.

Mowgli Keen Torin. Keen Torin. Fooder. Messua. Mowgli Wileboy. Keen Torin.

Messua Time for sleep. Sleep on bed.

(Mowgli stops motionless.)

What's wrong, Mowgli? Don't you like the hut?

Mowgli realises she looks troubled. He goes to her and touches her face.

Mowgli Mess-ua.

(He points to the bed.)

Mowgli Wileboy.

He points outside and mimes sleep.

Messua You sleep out there if you like. Goodnight Mowgli.

Mowgli Mowgli Wileboy.

He smiles and walks out of the hut. Messua lies down on the bed. Mowgli, outside, finds the knife in its hiding place, sniffs it and puts it back. He stubs his toe on the tin trunk. He gets down and sniffs the trunk but can't open it. He looks at stars and stretches and smiles. He lies down, like a baby with hands over his eyes.

Music and lights to indicate passage of time. The lights go up on Mowgli and Messua outside hut, having an English lesson.

Messua	Mowgli lives in India.
Mowgli	Yes. Mowgli lives in India.
Messua	And Queen Victoria lives in England.
Mowgli	Keen Toria live in England.
Messua	She is Queen of England and Queen of India too.
Mowgli	Is she Keen of Jungle too? No Mister Barnstaple Keen of Jungle, yes?

Buldeo strolls over.

Buldeo	Might as well teach monkeys to talk.
Mowgli	Monkeys talk same as you, Buldeo. But they look prettier.
Buldeo	Don't trust him too far, Messua. He's a wolf at heart.
Messua	Mowgli's a good boy.
Buldeo	Perhaps so … Messua – that tiger that stole your son.
Messua	Yes.
Buldeo	I saw him again last night, on the trail beside the Forest Officer's house.
Mowgli	What tiger, Buldeo?
Buldeo	A ghost-tiger.
Mowgli	Ghost?
Buldeo	There was a money-lender who lived in this village a few years ago. And his wicked ghost is this tiger. And I know that this is true because Purun Dass always limped from the blow that he got in a riot when his account-books were burned. And the tiger I speak of, he limps too, because his footprints are unequal.
Mowgli	That tiger limp because he was born lame. Everyone know Shere Khan was born lame. To talk of the soul of a money-lender in a beast that never had the courage of a jackal – that is child talk – that is cobweb and moon-talk.
Buldeo	Oh, the Jungle brat speaks with most eloquent

tongue now. You have taught him much, Messua, by kindness. Now I will teach him manners with a stick.

Buldeo grabs a piece of bamboo, but Mowgli dodges underneath it, dives and bites Buldeo in the ankle. Buldeo exits yelling.

Messua   Mowgli, you must calm down. You know much about the Jungle, perhaps Mr Barnstaple will give you a job.

Mowgli   No, Mowgli is a Wileboy.

Messua   You're not going to trouble Buldeo again are you?

Mowgli   No. No. Promise. I am going after bigger game – Shere Khan.

Scene Ten: Calico Pie

The verandah of the Forest Officer's house.

Mowgli walks by with his knife in his hand. Mr Barnstaple and Daisy are on the verandah. He is in a hammock, she in a chair with a large, oblong book. Mowgli stops to stare. They don't notice him.

Barnstaple   What's the book Daisy?

Daisy   'Nonsense', Papa, by Edward Lear.

Barnstaple   When are you going to grow up, Daisy Barnstaple?

Daisy   I don't know Papa.

Barnstaple   Your dear Mother would have wished you to spend more time on your Bible and less upon the silly nonsense of Mr Lear.

Daisy   She would, Papa.

Barnstaple   Good girl. Well, think I'd better go to bed. Remember – off to bed before the sun sinks behind the pineapples.

Daisy   Of course, Papa, happy dreams.

Barnstaple   Er, yes, happy dreams Daisy.

Daisy begins to sing from her book.

Daisy   Calico Pie,
         The little birds fly
         Down to the calico tree,
         Their wings were blue
         And they sang 'Tilly-loo'!
         Till away they flew –
         And they never came back to me!
             They never came back
             They never came back
         They never came back to me!

         Calico Jan,
         The little fish swam
         Over the Syllabub Sea,
         He took off his hat
         To the sole and the sprat
         And the willaby-wat,
         But he never came back to me!
             He never came back
             He never came back
         He never came back to me!

         Calico Dan,
         The little mice ran,
         To be ready in time for tea,
         Flippity plup,
         They drank it all up
         And danced in the cup –
         But they never came back to me!
             They never came back
             They never came back
         They never came back to me!

         Calico Drum
         The grasshoppers come,
         The butterfly, beetle and bee,
         Over the ground
         Around and around
         With a hop and a bound –
         But they never came back to me!
             They never came back

> They never came back
> They never came back to me!

Daisy closes the book and exits as if into the house. Mowgli watches her go.

Mowgli Goodnight, Daisy Barnstaple.

Mowgli lopes off along the trail . . .

Scene Eleven: Tiger Tiger

The Jungle. Akela is lying dead on the ground. Tabaqui the jackal is stalking towards him. Just as he stoops to lick the blood, Mowgli is astride Tabaqui and holding the knife to his throat.

Mowgli Tabaqui the Dish-Licker! What have you done?

Tabaqui Nothing, nothing, I have done nothing, O most powerful Manling.

Mowgli And is it nothing to have murdered Akela, the wise old wolf who led our Pack so many years?

Tabaqui Truly, O monstrously strong one, I did not kill Akela. But I smelled his blood from beyond the Council Rock and I could not help coming to pay my respects.

Mowgli The lapping of blood and the gnawing of bones – these are fine respects. Tabaqui?

Tabaqui Yes, Mowgli.

Mowgli I have grown a new claw, you see.

Tabaqui Yes, Mowgli.

Mowgli It is a very terrible claw, Tabaqui.

Tabaqui Yes, Mowgli.

Mowgli And it will tear open your throat if you do not tell me who killed Akela.

Tabaqui It was my master, it was Shere Khan.

Mowgli And the blood of Akela is on your lips also. Die a jackal's death.

(Mowgli cuts Tabaqui's throat. Then he gives a great call.)

Baloo, Grey Brother, Bagheera, Kaa!

Bagheera and Baloo, take our great old friend Akela to the burial place. I shall take revenge tonight. Shere Khan shall pay for this death, just as Tabaqui has paid.

Grey Brother   Tabaqui was a jackal, a coward, a puny vampire. But Shere Khan is a tiger and his strength is terrible.

Bagheera   His strength indeed is very great. And yet his brain is not so great.

Baloo returns with Kaa.

Baloo   Oh, Mowgli, even if we all fell upon Shere Khan at once, he would overwhelm us.

Kaa   It is true little Brother.

Mowgli   My friends, you forget that I have been living amongst men. And I have learned some of the cunning ways of men. And men have a deadly game they play with tigers.

Grey Brother   Let us play that game, Mowgli.

Mowgli   It is good. All of you, take some of the blood of Tabaqui and sprinkle it on the trails leading to this clearing.

(They do.)

Here in this hollow tree, there lies a pool of birdlime. We take one of the broad leaves of the Prauss tree, like this. And we smear it with the birdlime, like this. And then we lay the leaf on the mangey corpse, like this.

(Mowgli places a leaf on Tabaqui.)

And then we smear another leaf and then another leaf.

(They all perform this operation and form a pile of leaves.)

And then we wait . . .

(A roar is heard.)

So soon, Shere Khan. Look the pools of Tabaqui's blood are growing black with ants.

Baloo I do not see how a tiger . . .

Mowgli A tiger is simply a great cat. And the family of cats hate to have anything stuck on their paws. Now friends, pretend to be frightened and retreat from Shere Khan. But wait among the trees and watch his death.

Shere Khan enters.

Shere Khan What is happening here? A council? A plot?

Mowgli No plot, mighty Shere Khan. We heard a cry, a jackal's cry and came to see who had died.

Baloo But we could find no corpse.

Shere Khan I smell the dead one now. I know that smell.

Kaa Shall we leave you, Oh mighty one?

Shere Khan Yes, I smell the place.

(The others stand well back as Shere Khan noses the pile of leaves which covers Tabaqui.)

It is my servant Tabaqui the Dish-Licker. Oh somebody will pay for this death.

Shere Khan has a leaf stuck on a front paw. He tries to wipe it off against his face. It sticks to his face and he puts his paw down on another sticky leaf. This begins to annoy him. But every time he tries to wipe off another leaf, another sticks on him. He rolls in leaves in his fury and finally he is so covered by them that he can't see. He lies still. Mowgli whispers.

Mowgli Now he cannot see, so now he lies still. And now I move in with my terrible claw.

(Mowgli goes to the leaf covered figure and stabs and stabs again. He shouts as he stabs.)

Akela! Akela! Akela!

(Mowgli stands up.)

Brothers, that was a dog's death. His hide will look well on the Council Rock. Come join me, we must work quickly. Let us skin him.

Mowgli and his friends tug and tear at the hide and peel off leaves. Suddenly Buldeo is approaching, carrying a gun. The animals drop out of sight.

Buldeo   What is this? To think you can skin a tiger! It is the lame tiger too, and there is a hundred rupees reward for his death. Well, well, perhaps I will give you one of the rupees when I have taken the skin to Mr Barnstaple. Let me see where are my flint and steel? I must burn the tiger's whiskers so his ghost will not dare haunt me.

Buldeo stoops down with his flint.

Mowgli   Hm! So you will take the hide to Mr Barnstaple for the reward and perhaps give me one rupee? I need that skin for my own use. Hey – take away that fire!

Buldeo   What talk is this to the chief hunter of the village? Your luck and the stupidity of the tiger have helped you to the kill. You cannot even skin him properly, little beggar-brat, and you dare to tell me, Buldeo, not to singe his whiskers. Mowgli, I will not give you any of the reward, but only a very big beating. Leave the carcass.

Mowgli   By the bull that bought me and by Keen Toria of England, must I stay babbling to an old ape all day? Here, Grey Brother, this man annoys me.

(*Grey Brother leaps. He knocks Buldeo to the ground and stands over him.*)

You are altogether right, Buldeo. You will never give me any of the reward. There is an old war between this lame tiger and myself – a very old war, and – I have won.

Buldeo lying very still, speaks to himself.

Buldeo   Maybe this is sorcery.

(*Buldeo speaks to Mowgli.*)

Maharajah! O great king!

Mowgli keeps on skinning.

Mowgli Yes.

Buldeo I did not know that you were anything more than a wild boy. May I get up and go away, or will your servant treat me to pieces?

Mowgli Go, and peace go with you. Let him go Grey Brother. But another time, do not meddle with my game.

Scene Twelve: A Hero's Welcome

The village. Two Villagers and the Priest are joined by Buldeo in blowing horns, ringing bells and any old bit of tin. Riotous noise of village in uproar. Mowgli approaches, with Grey Brother at his heels, tiger skin on his shoulder.

Mowgli What fine music. They are all out to greet me as a hero because I have killed Shere Khan. Greetings my friends.

Priest Wolf. Wolf's cub. Go away.

Buldeo It is he. He has a demon wolf at his side even now.

Grey Brother The man is rude. A demon.

1st Villager Sorcerer. Wolf's brat. Jungle demon.

Mowgli Let us go Grey Brother.

Messua I do not believe them. But go away or they will kill you. Buldeo says you are a wizard. But I know you have avenged the death of my son.

1st Villager Come back. Come back Messua, or we will stone you.

Mowgli Run back Messua. I have at least paid for your son's life. I am no wizard. When you can, go quietly to Mr Barnstaple and tell him everything. Farewell.

Messua Farewell.

Scene Thirteen: Mowgli's Song

The Council Rock. Grey Brother and Wolves, plus Bagheera and Baloo and Kaa all sit around. Mowgli enters wearing tiger skin.

Mowgli   Brothers and Sisters, they have cast me out from the Man-Pack. But I come with the hide of Shere Khan to keep my word. Look well, O Wolves!

The song of Mowgli – I, Mowgli, am singing. Let the Jungle listen to the things I have done.

Shere Khan said he would kill – would kill! At the gates in the twilight he would kill Mowgli the Frog!

He ate and he drank. Drink deep, Shere Khan, for when will you drink again? Sleep and dream of the kill.

I am alone in the Jungle, Bagheera, come to me! Come to me all my friends for there is big game afoot.

I have killed your servant Tabaqui, Shere Khan, and now he lies under the leaves of the Prauss tree.

Come to the funeral, Shere Khan, come to the funeral of your tame jackal, the Licker of Dishes.

And then he came, the Lame One appeared, but the leaves of the Prauss tree stuck to his paws and his anger flamed like a forest fire

And he was rolling in the leaves and he was covered in the leaves a tiger covered in leaves until he was blind and helpless

And he was blind and could not see the terrible claw that ripped open his throat and spilled his blood on the Jungle floor.

Ssh! He is asleep. We will not wake him, for his strength is very great. The kites have come down to see it. The black ants have come up to know it. There is a great assembly in his honour.

Alala! I have no cloth to wrap me. The kites will see that I am naked. I am ashamed to meet all these people.

Lend me your coat, Shere Khan. Lend me your fine

striped coat that I may go to the Council Rock.
Dance on the hide of Shere Khan, but my heart is
   very heavy. My mouth is cut and wounded with
   the stones from the village.
But my heart is very light because I have come back
   to the Jungle. Why?
These two things fight together in me as the snakes
   fight in the spring.
The water comes out of my eyes: yet I laugh while it
   falls. Why?
I am two Mowglis, but the hide of Shere Khan is
   under my feet.
All the Jungle knows that I have killed Shere Khan.
   Look – look well, O wolves
Ahae! My heart is heavy with the things that I do not
   understand.

Look well, O Wolves. Have I kept my word?

All wolves   (*Howling in harmony.*) Yes!
Grey Brother   Lead us, O Mowgli.
Bagheera   No, that may not be. When you have fed you will
wish to cast out the Man-cub again. You are called
the Free People. You fought for freedom, and it is
yours. Eat it, O Wolves.

Mowgli   Man-Pack and Wolf-Pack have cast me out. Now I will
hunt alone in the Jungle.

Mowgli exits.

Scene Fourteen: The Interview

The verandah of the Forest Officer's house. Evening.
Mr Barnstaple in evening dress, enjoying a drink.
Daisy embroidering beside him. The sun setting.

Daisy   Father, why did you send for the wild boy?
Barnstaple   Three reasons. One, he intrigues me. He's out of his

time – he has been living before the Iron Age, before the Stone Age. Look, he is at the beginning of the history of man – Adam in the Garden. Second reason. The natives think that he summoned the elephants, and deer and assorted wild game to tear the village apart. I want to get to the bottom of that.

Daisy It's nonsense, though. How could he tell elephants what to do?

Barnstaple I don't know, Daisy. You see, Mowgli was brought up in the Jungle and taught by wild animals in the Jungle. I was brought up in Guildford and taught by wild animals at Harrow.

Daisy And what's the third reason you want to see him?

Barnstaple I want to offer him a job.

Mowgli appears. He has selected the finest items from the tin trunk and has managed to put them on. On top of it all he wears a crown. The clothes are not so much silly, as wrong. Wrong in size and shape and in relation to each other. But he does retain a sort of dignity.

Mowgli Greetings, Mister Barnstaple. Greetings, Daisy Barnstaple.

Barnstaple Mowgli, I have heard bad words about you from the people of the village.

Mowgli They have bad tongues, what can they say besides bad words?

Barnstaple They say – and I know this is ridiculous – that you summoned wild animals out of the Jungle and ordered them to tear down the village.

Mowgli Yes, that is right.

Barnstaple You admit it?

Mowgli Of course. It is true.

Barnstaple Why?

Mowgli Because they were going to burn a woman to death. The woman Messua, who has been good to me when I first came among man.

Barnstaple   Mowgli, don't make fun of me.

Mowgli   Make fun?

Barnstaple   You can no more summon wild animals than I can call a London policeman from the Jungle.

Mowgli   Oh? Bagheera! Baloo! Come and show your noble and beautiful faces to the Forest Officer Sahib.

Bagheera and Baloo walk by the verandah like troops past a saluting base and exit. Barnstaple pours himself another drink. Daisy smiles.

Barnstaple   It's uncanny. Listen. I am Forest Officer for the Department of Woods and Forests. This is my Jungle.

Mowgli   Oh. Do they number the trees and blades of grass here?

Barnstaple   They do. In case such beggars as you steal them.

Mowgli   I would not hurt the Jungle.

Barnstaple   Mowgli – I offer you this job, to stop wandering up and down the Jungle and driving beasts to tear villages apart, and to live in this Jungle as a Forest Guard. You will drive the Villagers' goats away when there is no order to feed them in the Jungle. You will admit those goats when there is such an order. You will keep down the boar and the deer when they become too many. You will tell me how and where the tigers are moving that I may shoot them, and what game is in the forest. You will give me warning of all fires in the Jungle. And for this work there is a payment every month in silver. And at the end, when you have got a wife and cattle and – maybe, children – a pension. What is your answer?

Mowgli   I will not tell you everything in the Jungle. I will not tell you where my friends are and what they do. But the rest I can do. We will kill many tigers, yes? And you pay me?

Barnstaple   Queen Victoria will pay you.

(*He gives him a coin.*)

That is her picture.

Mowgli looks delighted.

Mowgli   Oh. Keen Toria! Keen Toria! For this picture I will work for many moons.

Barnstaple   There will be more pictures.

Mowgli   I want no more pictures. I want only one wish.

Barnstaple   Of course, Mowgli. Whatever you ask.

Mowgli   Then I ask for your daughter. I ask for Miss Daisy Barnstaple.

There is a pause.

Barnstaple   Go inside Daisy.

(Daisy goes into the house.)

Mowgli. My daughter will marry a gentleman.

Mowgli   I am not gentle with tigers. But I will be gentle with Daisy.

Barnstaple   You will never see Daisy again. Get back into the Jungle. You're not a man just because you've stolen a lot of ridiculous clothes that don't fit. You're an ape.

Mowgli   I am not an ape. I am a man.

Barnstaple   Listen boy, you are an ape in man's clothing.

(Barnstaple starts to laugh and he lets go with all the laughter he's been holding back because of – to him – Mowgli's absurd appearance. Mowgli is furious and runs off. Barnstaple turns back to the house.)

Daisy! Daisy?

(He looks into the house.)

Daisy, where are you? Daisy!

Scene Fifteen: The Spring Running

The Jungle. There is a full moon. Daisy is reading.

Daisy   The feeling of unhappiness he had never known

before covered him as water covers a log.

Mowgli appears on the other side of the Jungle. He is still in his clothes and crown. He throws down the crown.

Mowgli I have surely eaten poison. My strength has gone and soon I shall die. Now I am hot and now I am cold, and now I am neither hot nor cold, but angry with something I cannot see. Huhu! It is time to make a running. Yes I will make a spring running through the Jungle! Now!

Mowgli begins to run. As he runs, he casts of his 'civilised' clothes bit by bit until he is down to his loin cloth. Music plays.

Daisy It was a perfect white night, as they call it. All green things seemed to have made a month's growth since the morning. Forgetting his unhappiness, Mowgli sang aloud with pure delight as he settled into his stride.

(Mowgli begins to sing – wordlessly at first.)

It was more like flying than anything else, and the springy ground deadened the fall of his feet. A man-taught man would have stumbled through the moonlight, but Mowgli's muscles bore him up as though he were a feather. When a rotten log or a hidden stone turned under his foot he saved himself never changing his pace, without effort and without thought.

When he was tired of ground-going, he threw up his hands monkey-fashion to the nearest creeper, and seemed to float rather than to climb up into the thin branches, from where he would follow a tree-road until his mood changed, and he shot downward in a long leafy curve to the Jungle floor again.

Mowgli's wordless song coalesces into words. He begins to sing.

Mowgli Daisy Barnstaple! Daisy Barnstaple!

Daisy There were still, hot hollows surrounded by wet

rocks where he could hardly breathe for the heavy scents of the night flowers and the bloom along the creeper buds.

So he ran, sometimes shouting, sometimes singing to himself, the happiest thing in all the Jungle that night.

Mowgli stands face to face with Daisy. She drops her book. She stands and puts her arms round him. Blackout on them. Spotlight on Mr Barnstaple searching the Jungle for his daughter. He carries a gun.

Barnstaple Daisy! Where are you? If you can hear me – try to climb a tree and stay there till I find you. Daisy! If there's a tiger there, just keep facing him, stare him out. Don't turn your back – don't turn your back on a tiger. If it's a snake – stay still and scream for me. I've got my gun, Daisy!

Sudden pool of moonlight which reveals Daisy lying happily on the ground. Mowgli is playing 'Calico Pie' on a bamboo flute and his head is crowned with little white flowers. Barnstaple freezes as he spots them. Daisy begins to sing.

Daisy Calico Pie,
The little birds fly
Down to the calico tree,
Their wings were blue
And they sang 'Tilly-loo'
Till away they flew –
And they never came back to me!
    They never came back
    They never came back
They never came back to me!

Mowgli Daisy – there is a man standing behind me. Do not move.

Barnstaple Daisy, it's all right, I'm here! Daisy has he hurt you?

Daisy We love each other, Papa.

Barnstaple Daisy, will you come home with me now. As soon as

I've dealt with this savage little brute.

Mowgli Bagheera! Baloo! Kaa!

(As Barnstaple raises his rifle he is overwhelmed by a three-animal attack by Bagheera, Baloo and Kaa. Messua enters poling a small wooden boat along a stream.)

My friends. Messua! Daisy, this is Messua. Messua, this is Daisy Barnstaple.

Mowgli helps Daisy, with her suitcase, into the boat. He turns to his three friends.

Bagheera So this is the end of your trail, Little Brother.

Baloo Akela said it, that Mowgli should drive Mowgli back to the Man-Pack. I said it, too. But who listens to Baloo?

Kaa Man returns to man at last, though the Jungle does not cast him out.

Mowgli I would not leave you. But the Red Flower is in my body, my bones are water – and – I know not what I know. Hai-ail.

(Mowgli sobs.)

I don't want to go, but my feet draw me.

Bagheera Remember, Bagheera loved you!

Baloo You have heard. There is no more. Go now; but first come to me. O wise Little Frog, come to me.

Mowgli sobs as he embraces the bear.

Kaa It is hard to cast the skin.

Mowgli I go now. Deep into the Jungle. And perhaps beyond the Jungle. I go with my second mother. And I go with my mate. Farewell.

Mowgli steps into the boat which begins to move slowly away. Bagheera, Baloo and Kaa sing.

Man goes to man! Cry the challenge through the
    Jungle!
He that was our brother goes away.
Hear, now and judge, O you people of the Jungle –
Answer, who shall turn him – who shall stay?

Man goes to man! And he leaves us in the Jungle.
He that was our brother sorrows sore!
Man goes to man! Oh we loved him in the Jungle!
To the man-trail where we may not follow more!

The end.

QUESTIONS AND EXPLORATIONS

The Wild Animal Song Contest

1 Keeping Track

These questions are here to make you stop and think more carefully about what's happening in the play.

1 (Page 1) Read Debit's opening speech. It rhymes and is very rhythmical. Prepare a reading of this. You can interpret it in any way you want, perhaps as a rap. Now try writing your own rap.

2 (Page 2) Quilla is a golden eagle from the USA. Why do you think Adrian Mitchell chose to have an eagle representing America? Now consider why he decided on a bear to represent Russia and a lion for Britain.

3 (Page 4) Rogan, the lion says: 'I'm really meant to be King of the Beasts, noamin?' What does 'noamin' mean? Why is it written like this?

4 (Page 5) In the *Song Contest Song*, Artovsky says that if you don't like his song, he'll give you a friendly hug. Will it really be friendly? What would it do to you?

5 (Pages 6–7) The other contestants all make fun of Raffa. What is one of the main differences between a giraffe and a lion, an eagle or a bear (think about what they eat)? How might this affect the way they see things?

6 (Page 8) 'There's no such thing as sorry!' Why does Debit say this?

7 (Page 8) What purpose, if any, does Rule 2 of the contest

serve? What does it remind you of?

8   (Pages 10–11) What sort of impression do you get of Quilla when you read her song *When the Eagle Smiles?*

9   (Page 12) Debit tries to bribe Quilla, saying that she'll win the contest if only she gives him her eyes. Do you think she'll do this?

10   (Page 13) In Artovsky's first song he seems to contradict himself: 'I'm a bear of peace' and: 'And I march to war . . . I'm a fighting bear And I'll kill for peace.' What do you think of what he's saying?

11   (Page 13) His second song, *The Dancing Bear*, is very different. What does it tell you about Artovsky?

12   (Page 14) Now Debit tries to bribe the bear. From Artovsky he wants his teeth and claws. What do you think he might demand from Rogan the lion, and Raffa the giraffe?

13   (Page 16) Rogan in his song says that, although he prefers tinned cat food, he might still bite in half some young giraffe. Why do you think he might have chosen this example?

14   (Pages 18–19) Raffa insists that she must win the Million Gun, saying that if any of the others win 'they'll use it to murder us all'. Do you agree with her? Why might they act in this way?

15   (Page 19) What was in the note that Bonzo passed to Raffa?

16   (Pages 21–22) Why do all the contestants decide to drop out of the contest? What would be the problem with this decision and why do they decide to form a group?

17   (Pages 22–23) Read the song *Group a Group.*

(a) If you haven't heard of any of the groups mentioned, try to find out about them.

(b) Why are the lines: 'The sound of the Stones can make you stagger, But it wouldn't work if it was just Bill Wyman.' funny? What did you expect the second line to say?

(c) See if you can write a more up-to-date version of the song, using bands or singers that are around now.

18 (Pages 25–26) How is the song *New Lion* different to Rogan's original *Roaring Song* (Pages 15–16)?

19 (Page 27) Quilla and Artovsky sail around in a 'beautiful pea-green boat'. Can you remember where this line is taken from?

20 (Page 29) Debit claims that he will take the contest prize because all the contestants have broken the rules. Is that the real reason? Who do you think he would have awarded it to if the contest had carried on as it was supposed to do?

21 (Page 31) What is Debit's reaction to the break-up of the Million Gun? Would you trust him as part of the group?

2   Explorations

A   Issues

1 Debit says there must be no 'political songs about famine, unemployment or peace'. What do you think the representatives from the four countries would have to say about these issues? Do you know any examples of this sort of song?

2 It's in the rules that the animals need to wear human masks to 'add dignity to the proceedings'. Why is this? Do you agree that the animals would look more dignified dressed as people?

3 Can you think of any examples when humans 'dress up' animals to look like humans? Do the animals look 'dignified' in these situations?

4 'You can't all win. You've got to compete. You've got to fight each other. That's the way progress gets made.' says Debit. Do you agree with this? What alternative does the play present to competition?

5 Raffa says: 'We'll be a group. Nobody could beat us then.' (Page 21)

Compare the song that follows *Group a Group* with Debit's *The Land of War* song. (Pages 24–25.) Which one do you believe in?

6 The play ends on an optimistic note. Do you feel hopeful about the future of our planet, and the animals and people that inhabit it?

B Casting

Each time a play is put on to the stage, actors need to be carefully chosen to take on the various roles. This is usually done by the director meeting lots of actors at auditions. To make their jobs easier, directors will make notes to remind them exactly what they're looking for from the actors.

Imagine that you're a director. Think carefully about all the different characters in the play and make casting notes on them. Think about:

What sort of voice and accent each character needs.
What kind of personality needs to be put across.
What does the character need to look like (gender, age,
physical looks, etc.).

C Accents

Everyone has an accent. Your accent is simply the way you
pronounce the words you speak. As the animals in the play
are from different nations it's important that the actors work
hard to get the accent right.

1   Choose a speech by each of the contestants. Read it
    aloud, emphasising the appropriate accent:
        Quilla from the USA.
        Artovsky from Russia.
        Raffa from Africa.

    (There are many different American, Russian and African
    accents – just try one you are familiar with).
        Rogan from London (cockney).

2   What sort of accent do you think Debit would have?

D Creation myths

In Raffa's song she tells how the giraffe was created. There are
many imaginary accounts of how various creatures came to
be. Look at Ted Hughes' *How the Whale Became and Other
Stories*, Kipling's *Just So Stories* or read Aesop's *Fables.*

Now try to make up your own imaginary accounts of how
different animals developed their unique characteristics.

GLOSSARY

comrade	colleague or friend. A term particularly used by socialists and communists.
dignity	respect
leonine	lion-like
menagerie	a collection of wild animals in cages
proceedings	the business done at a meeting
superfluous	more than enough

Mowgli's Jungle

1 Keeping Track

These questions are here to help you think more carefully about what's happening in the play. Answer them as you read through it.

Scene 1

1 Why does the woman roll her baby into the entrance of the cave before running away from the tiger?

Scene 2

1 The baby is described as a man-*cub*. Why do the wolves call him this?

2 Mother Wolf says: 'Now the villagers are angry with (Shere Khan).
Why are they angry? What will this mean for the rest of the animals of the Jungle?

3 Shere Khan says: 'Each dog barks in his own yard!'
What does he mean by this?

4 Why do you think Mother Wolf calls Mowgli a 'little frog'?

Scene 3

1 Why do the wolves call themselves the 'Free People'?

2 Who objects to Mowgli being accepted into the Pack and who supports him?

3 How are the wolves eventually persuaded to allow him into the Pack?

4 Akela says of Mowgli: 'He may be able to help us one day.'
In what possible way could a boy be of use to a pack of wolves? What special skills will he have that they have not?

Scene 4

1. Mowgli has many rules to learn and laws to follow (take a look at the Hunting Verse and The Wood and Water Laws). Why does Baloo insist so strongly that Mowgli learns all the Laws of the Jungle?

2. How will the Master-words help Mowgli?

3. Why does Bagheera think Mowgli might be threatened by his own tribe? Which tribe might he be thinking of?

4. When Baloo says: 'The pity of the Monkey-People! The stillness of the mountain stream! The cool of the summer sun!'
What does he mean? Why is he talking in this way?

5. Why does Mowgli leave his friends for the monkeys?

6. Why does Bagheera keep telling Kaa what the monkeys call him?

Scene 5

1. Judging by their songs and the way they speak, what impression have you formed of the monkeys? In what ways do they differ from the other animals? (Compare this ceremony with the Rock Council of the wolves.)

2. Do the monkeys really intend to make Mowgli their king to rule over them? If not, what do you think they might do to him?

3. The city of the Cold Lairs has been uninhabited by people for a long time. Can you see anything in this scene which explains why?

Scene 6

1. The Fat One and Wild Sister are very discontented at the beginning of this scene. Why and who do they blame?

2　Why do you think Shere Kahn is being so sympathetic?

3　Shere Khan says that he will soon 'drink the blood from [Mowgli's] throat and tear the heart from his chest'. Why hasn't he done this before and why does he think he will be able to do it now?

4　What is Bagheera's explanation for why some of the wolves have turned against Mowgli?

5　It is possible to work out Mowgli's age from this scene. How old is he?

Scene 7

1　What does the 'red flower' turn out to be?

2　Why is it described so?

Scene 8

1　'You know how the plot was made . . . it was cleverly done'.
　　What does Akela mean by this?

2　Who plotted against Akela and why?

3　Mowgli says: 'When next I come to the Council Rock, it will be with Shere Khan's hide on my head.'
　　Yet a few scenes earlier, Shere Khan vowed: 'Before the moon changes, I will drink the blood from [Mowgli's] throat, and tear the heart from his chest'.
　　Who do you think will win?

4　Why does Mowgli ask Bagheera if he, Mowgli, is dying?

Scene 9

1　Look at the Villagers' first reactions to Mowgli. Are there any similarities between these and the reactions of the wolves when they first came across the baby Mowgli?

2　What does 1st Villager think of Buldeo?

3   When the Priest asks which language they should teach Mowgli, Mr Barnstaple says 'English of course'. Given that the play is set in India, why does he say that?

4   As Mowgli goes to sleep, 'music and lights indicate the passage of time'. How much time do you think might have passed before the final part of the scene?

Scene 10

1   What does Mr Barnstaple think of Daisy's choice of reading?

2   What does it tell you about Daisy?

3   What do you think might have happened to Daisy's mother?

Scene 11

1   What is Mowgli's new 'claw'?

2   Shere Khan has killed Akela. Why is this such a terrible thing?

3   What has Mowgli learned from the humans, that will help him to outwit Shere Khan?

4   Mowgli realises that he could get 100 rupees for the skin of Shere Khan. Why does he not claim this? What does he want to do instead?

Scene 12

1   Scene 12 is called 'A Hero's Welcome' but Mowgli is not treated like a hero; he is shocked at the Villagers' reaction to him. Why do they react in this way?

Scene 13

1   In the second verse of his song, Mowgli describes his confused feelings. What is he confused about and why?

2 Why does Bagheera say that Mowgli cannot lead the wolves?

Scene 14

1 Something has happened in the village between Scene 12 when the Villagers cast Mowgli out and this scene. What is it?

2 Why did it happen?

3 Why does Barnstaple offer Mowgli this job? Is it just because he knows the Jungle so well?

Scene 15

1 What book do you think Daisy is reading from?

2 Baloo says 'Akela said it, that Mowgli should drive Mowgli back to the Man-Pack'. What do you think Akela meant by this?

3 'It is hard to take off the skin', says Kaa. What skin is Mowgli taking off?

2 Explorations

A Characters

1 In Scene 4, Baloo and Bagheera react very differently to Mowgli's cheekiness and his kidnap by the Bandar-log monkeys. Read carefully through the scene again and note down what you think the scene shows about the bear and the panther.

2 From Scene 8 onwards Mowgli is referred to as 'wise' by his Jungle friends. Why do they call him this? What do you think they mean by it?

3   Throughout *Mowgli's Jungle,* Mowgli is seen first as a man in the animal kingdom, then as a wild savage in man's society (he is called an 'ape' by Barnstaple, a 'wolf's brat' and a 'jungle demon' by the Villagers). At times he just doesn't seem to fit in anywhere. As Mowgli himself says: 'Man-Pack and Wolf-Pack have cast me out.' Where do you think Mowgli really belongs? Does his situation improve by the end of the play?

4   In Scene 14, Daisy says nothing while her father is talking to Mowgli. Track her thoughts while they are speaking. Two people read the dialogue while the third says Daisy's thoughts aloud.

5   We are not told at the end of the play what happens to Mr Barnstaple. Imagine an extra scene where he returns to his house without Daisy. What would be his view of Mowgli and the Jungle? What would be the reaction of the Villagers?

B Themes

1   How are the worlds of people and animals, as shown in *Mowgli's Jungle* different and how are they similar?

2   Writers have always been fascinated with the relationship between so-called 'civilized' people and wild animals. In addition to the *Jungle Book* stories, there's the Roman story of *Romulus and Remus* and Edgar Rice Burroughs' 'Tarzan' books (along with many 'Tarzan' films). Can you think of any other examples? Why do you think people are so interested in this subject?

3   Barnstaple says in Scene 14: 'This is my Jungle.'

Who else throughout the play thinks that the Jungle belongs to them? What happens to the characters who 'own' the Jungle?

C Staging the play

This play is a challenge to put on to the stage. Not only are most of the characters animals (including birds and a 30 foot long python!), but you also have to represent a jungle, with Mowgli and monkeys swinging through the trees.

In groups take a few scenes each and plan how you would stage them. Think first about the animals:

What would you use for the costumes?

What use would you make of puppets or masks?

How will you research the different ways animals walk and move?

Then think about the setting and objects needed in the play:

How will you represent the Jungle?

It would be unsafe to have a real fire on the stage, so how would you represent the 'red flower' that the animals talk of?

D The book of the play

1 *Mowgli's Jungle* is based on Kipling's story *The Jungle Book* written in 1894. Daisy is reading from the book in Scene 15.

Reproduce a piece of text from the original to compare with a scene or scenes from the play. Ask questions about the changes that have been made to dramatise it effectively. Compare the language used.

2   Watch and listen to the songs from Walt Disney's *The Jungle Book* on video (called *Songs of the South*). How do they differ from *Mowgli's Jungle?* (They are also obtainable on record and cassette.)
    Which do you prefer – the songs of the play or of the film? Give reasons for your choice.

3   In Scene 15 of *Mowgli's Jungle,* Daisy Barnstaple is reading 'The Spring Running' from Kipling's *Second Jungle Book.* As she reads it we see Mowgli acting out what she describes. Read this passage from the opening chapter of *The Jungle Book* and then red Scene 15 of *Mowgli's Jungle* again.

'Man!' he snapped. 'A man's cub. Look!'

Directly in front of him, holding on by a low branch, stood a naked brown baby who could just walk – as soft and as dimpled a little atom as ever came to a wolf's cave at night. He looked up into Father Wolf's face, and laughed.

'Is that a man's cub?' said Mother Wolf. 'I have never seen one. Bring it here.'

A wolf accustomed to moving his own cubs can, if necessary, mouth an egg without breaking it, and though Father Wolf's jaws closed right on the child's back not a tooth even scratched the skin, as he laid it down among the cubs.

'How little! How naked, and – how bold!' said Mother Wolf softly. The baby was pushing his way between the cubs to get close to the warm hide. *'Ahai!* He is taking his meal with the others. And so this is a man's cub. Now, was there ever a wolf that could boast of a man's cub among her children?'

'I have heard now and again of such a thing, but never in our Pack or in my time,' said Father Wolf. 'He is altogether without hair, and I could kill him with a touch of my foot. But see, he looks up and is not afraid.'

The moonlight was blocked out of the mouth of the cave, for Shere Khan's great square head and shoulders were thrust into the entrance.

Tabaqui, behind him, was squeaking: 'My lord, my lord, it went in here!'

'Shere Khan does us great honour,' said Father Wolf, but his eyes were very angry. 'What does Shere Khan need?'

'My quarry. A man's cub went this way,' said Shere Khan. 'Its parents have run off. Give it to me.'

Shere Khan had jumped at a woodcutter's camp-fire, as Father Wolf had said, and was furious from the pain of his burned feet. But Father Wolf knew that the mouth of the cave was too narrow for a tiger to come in by. Even where he was, Shere Khan's shoulders and forepaws were cramped for want of room, as a man's would be if he tried to fight in a barrel.

'The Wolves are a free people,' said Father Wolf. 'They take orders from the Head of the Pack, and not from any striped cattle-killer. The man's cub is ours – to kill if we choose.'

'Ye choose and ye do not choose! What talk is this of choosing? By the bull that I killed, am I to stand nosing into your dog's den for my fair dues? It is I, Shere Khan, who speak!'

The tiger's roar filled the cave with thunder. Mother Wolf shook herself clear of the cubs and sprang forward, her eyes, like two green moons in the darkness, facing the blazing eyes of Shere Khan.

'And it is I, Raksha [The Demon], who answer. The man's cub is mine, Lungri – mine to me! He shall not be killed. He shall live to run with the Pack and to hunt with the Pack; and in the end, look you, hunter of little naked cubs – frog-eater – fish-killer – he shall hunt *thee!* Now get hence, or by the Sambhur that I killed (*I* eat no starved cattle), back thou goest to thy mother, burned beast of the Jungle, lamer than ever thou camest into the world! Go!'

Father Wolf looked on amazed. He had almost forgotten the days when he won Mother Wolf in fair fight from five other wolves, when she ran in the Pack and was not called The Demon for compliment's sake. Shere Khan might have faced Father Wolf, but he could not stand up against Mother Wolf, for he knew that where he was she had all the advantage of the ground, and would fight to the death. So he backed out of the cave-mouth growling, and when he was clear he shouted:

'Each dog barks in his own yard! We will see what the Pack will say to this fostering of man-cubs. The cub is mine, and to my teeth he will come in the end, O bush-tailed thieves!

Mother Wolf threw herself down panting among the cubs, and Father Wolf said to her gravely:

'Shere Khan speaks this much truth. The cub must be shown to the Pack. Wilt thou still keep him, Mother?'

'Keep him!' she gasped. 'He came naked, by night, alone and very hungry; yet he was not afraid! Look, he has pushed one of my babes to one side already. And that lame butcher would have killed him and would have run off to the Waingunga while the villagers here hunted through all our lairs in revenge! Keep him? Assuredly I will keep him. Lie still, little frog. O thou Mowgli – for Mowgli the Frog I will call thee – the time will come when thou wilt hunt Shere Khan as he has hunted thee.'

What changes have been made to dramatise the original? What are the differences in the language used? Now try adapting all or some of the following passage, called 'Kaa's Hunting', for performance. Be aware of the tone and mood of the person speaking and what they are doing. Try to capture the spirit of excitement and adventure in the original.

The moon was sinking behind the hills, and the lines of trembling monkeys huddled together on the walls and battlements looked like ragged, shaky fringes of things. Baloo went down to the tank for a drink, and Bagheera began to put his fur in order, as Kaa glided out into the centre of the terrace and brought his jaws together with a ringing snap that drew all the monkeys' eyes upon him.

'The moon sets,' he said. 'Is there yet light to see?'

From the walls came a moan like a wind in the tree-tops: 'We see, O Kaa.'

'Good. Begins now the Dance – the Dance of the Hunger of Kaa. Sit still and watch.'

He turned twice or thrice in a big circle, weaving his head from right to left. Then he began making loops and figures of eight with his body, and soft, oozy triangles that melted into squares and five-sided figures, and coiled mounds, never resting, never hurrying, and never stopping his low, humming song. It grew darker and darker, till at last the dragging, shifting coils disappeared, but they could hear the rustle of the scales.

Baloo and Bagheera stood still as stone, growling in their throats, their neck-hair bristling, and Mowgli watches and wondered.

'*Bandar-log*,' said the voice of Kaa at last, 'can ye stir foot or hand without my order? Speak!'

'Without thy order we cannot stir foot or hand, O Kaa!'

'Good! Come all one pace closer to me.'

The lines of the monkeys swayed forward helplessly, and Baloo and Bagheera took one stiff step forward with them.

'Closer!' hissed Kaa, and they all moved again.

Mowgli laid his hands on Baloo and Bagheera to get them away, and the two great beasts started as though they had been waked from a dream.

'Keep thy hand on my shoulder,' Bagheera whispered. 'Keep it there, or I must go back – must go back to Kaa. *Aah!*'

'It is only old Kaa making circles in the dust,' said Mowgli; 'let us go'; and the three slipped off through a gap in the walls to the Jungle.

'*Whoof!*' said Baloo, when he stood under the still trees again. 'Never more will I make an ally of Kaa,' and he shook himself all over.

'He knows more than we,' said Bagheera, trembling. 'In a little time, had I stayed, I should have walked down his throat.'

'Many will walk by that road before the moon rises again,' said Baloo. 'He will have good hunting – after his own fashion.'

'But what was the meaning of it all?' said Mowgli, who did not know anything of a python's powers of fascination. 'I saw no more than a big snake making foolish circles till the dark came. And his nose was all sore. Ho! Ho!'

'Mowgli,' said Bagheera angrily, 'his nose was sore on *thy* account; as my ears and sides and paws and Baloo's neck and shoulders are bitten on *thy* account. Neither Baloo nor Bagheera will be able to hunt with pleasure for many days.'

'It is nothing,' said Baloo; 'we have the Man-cub again.'

'True; but he has cost us heavily in time which might have been spent in good hunting, in wounds, in hair – I am half plucked along my back – and, last of all, in honour. For, remember, Mowgli, I, who am the Black Panther, was forced to call upon Kaa for protection, and Baloo and I were both made stupid as little birds by the Hunger-Dance. All this, Man-cub, came of thy playing with the *Bandar-log.*'

'True; it is true,' said Mowgli sorrowfully. 'I am an evil Man-cub, and my stomach is sad in me.'

'*Mf!* What says the Law of the Jungle, Baloo?'

Baloo did not wish to bring Mowgli into any more trouble, but he could not tamper with the Law, so he mumbled: 'Sorrow never stays punishment. But remember, Bagheera, he is very little.'

'I will remember; but he has done mischief, and blows must be dealt now. Mowgli, has thou anything to say?'

'Nothing. I did wrong. Baloo and thou are wounded. It is just.'

Bagheera gave him half a dozen love-taps; from a panther's point of view they would hardly have waked one of his own cubs, but for a seven-year-old boy they amounted to as severe a beating as you could wish to avoid. When it was all over Mowgli sneezed, and picked himself up without a word.

'Now,' said Bagheera, 'jump on my back, Little Brother, and we will go home.'

One of the beauties of Jungle Law is that punishment settles all scores. There is no nagging afterwards.

Mowgli laid his head down on Bagheera's back and slept so deeply that he never waked when he was put down by Mother Wolf's side in the home-cave.

GLOSSARY

astride	with a leg on each side
batman	an officer's servant
birdlime	a sticky material painted on to twigs to trap small birds
blood brother	a form of close friendship made by two people mixing some of their blood, usually by cutting their thumbs
byre	a cowshed or other secluded place
cast the skin	what a snake does to shed its skin
Cold Lairs	the ruined city of the Bandar-log monkeys
council	a group that meets regularly to advise and rule
cower	to hide in fear
cowherd	a person who looks after cattle
creeper	a vine
Cupid's bow	the bow and arrow of the Roman God of love represented by a naked winged boy; also the upper lip shaped like the bow itself
customs	laws of a country
debt	something (often money) that is owed
deny	refuse
dignity	a proper way (of doing something)
doe	a female deer
dried well	an empty water source
eloquent	good use of language
ere	before
feebler	weaker
festoon	a chain of flowers, ribbons, leaves or lights
fin	an organ used by fish for movement

flint steel	an object that produces fire
flit	move lightly or quickly
flung	thrown
foliage	leaves
folly	a mistake or error
for many moons	for several months
fostering	to bring up a child that is not yours by birth
furlong sheer	a steep distance approximately 220 yards long
girdle	something that surrounds another object
give house room to	make space for or live with
glade	open space in the jungle
go forth	move forward
Harrow	English public school
haunch	a leg or thigh of an animal
hide	the skin of an animal
hypnotic	something or someone who can put you to sleep and make you do things they want you to do while you are asleep
kite	a soaring bird of prey, with long wings and a forked tail
knickerbockers	loose fitting trousers, gathered at the knees
jabbering	talking quickly, indistinctly or with little sense
jackal	a wild dog-like mammal which hunts in packs
lair	a resting place, den or hiding place
lame	unable to walk normally because of a problem with or injury to a leg
lash	to tie up
leaveth	leave behind
loin cloth	a cloth worn round the waist
lolling	hanging out
low	a sound made by cattle; a moo
lumber up	move in a slow, clumsy, noisy way

Maharajah	an Indian title meaning Great King or Prince
maimed	injured
mangey	a form of abuse meaning covered in skin disease
mango	a fleshy yellowish-red fruit
outcast	someone who is cast out from a group
pack	a group or formation
pawpaws	a melon-shaped fruit with orange flesh
pension	regular payment to people who have retired from work
pledge	promise
praying mantis	a large insect that holds its forelegs in a prayerlike position, while waiting to pounce on its prey
precede	to go before
predicate	to affirm, to state that something is true
pss-haw!	an expression of contempt or impatience
puny	weak
python	a large snake that crushes its prey
quarry	victims, usually of birds of prey
Queen Victoria	ruler of England and the British Empire 1837–1901
red flower	fire
revenge	getting your own back for an offence or injury
rupees	the money currency of India
sahib	a term of respect given in India
scale	the skin of fish or reptiles
scholar	a person who studies
scorch	burn
score	twenty
scorn	contempt
scumfish	a dirty or imperfect fish

sinister	evil or villainous
slivered	Kipling's expression meaning broken into pieces probably by lightning
sorcery	magic powers
spate	sudden river flood
spates	a flooded river
stalks	to slowly, secretly, and silently follow prey, preparing for a good moment to spring
talon	a claw of a bird
thicket	tangle of shrubs or trees
thine	yours
tuft	a piece of skin or hair
tusk	a long pointed tooth, or elephant's tusk
uncanny	mysterious
veer	to turn, change direction
verandah	a covered area outside a house
wake	the ripple left behind in water after something has passed through it. Also used generally to mean things left behind by someone or something passing through.
wallows	rolls about in mud, sand or water. A place used by buffalo, etc, for wallowing.
withered	dry and shrivelled